## "Libby, he's my son also"

Libby felt a wave of despair flow over her. "For how long would you play father? As long as it suits you?"

"It will always suit me. You think I'd walk out on him?"

Libby shook her head. "You walked out on me."

For a moment he just stared at her, a muscle working in his jaw. Then he raked savage fingers through his hair. "I'm back. I had a child with you, and I have the right to be his father."

"What are you going to do then, Alec? Try to take him from me?" She flung it at him as a challenge, then she looked at him, horrified. "You can't take him from me." She sounded desperate, and she knew it.

Alec sighed, a fire flickering in his eyes. "I don't know what I can do yet. But I'm going to do something."

American author **ANNE McALLISTER** majored in Spanish literature, has a master's degree in theology, copyedited textbooks and ghostwrote sermons. She might never have pursued her earlier interest in writing if a friend hadn't challenged her to write a Harlequin Romance. She has successfully met the challenge with many popular novels in Harlequin's Romance, Presents and American lines. She regards herself as blessed with a "terrifically tolerant husband" and "four opinionated but equally supportive children." In all her stories she writes about relationships—how they grow and how they challenge the people who share them.

## Books by Anne McAllister

### HARLEQUIN PRESENTS
844—LIGHTNING STORM
1060—TO TAME A WOLF
1099—THE MARRIAGE TRAP
1257—ONCE A HERO
1371—OUT OF BOUNDS

### HARLEQUIN ROMANCE
2721—DARE TO TRUST

### HARLEQUIN AMERICAN ROMANCE
186—BODY AND SOUL*
202—DREAM CHASERS
234—MARRY SUNSHINE
275—GIFTS OF THE SPIRIT
309—SAVING GRACE
341—IMAGINE
387—I THEE WED

*THE QUICKSILVER SERIES

# ANNE MCALLISTER

## island interlude

*Harlequin Books*

TORONTO • NEW YORK • LONDON
AMSTERDAM • PARIS • SYDNEY • HAMBURG
STOCKHOLM • ATHENS • TOKYO • MILAN
MADRID • WARSAW • BUDAPEST • AUCKLAND

Harlequin Presents first edition May 1992
ISBN 0-373-11459-1

Original hardcover edition published in 1991
by Mills & Boon Limited

ISLAND INTERLUDE

# CHAPTER ONE

'I GOT somethin' to tell you.'

'And I've got tons to tell you, too, Maddy.' Libby flung her arms around the older woman who had come hurrying down the broad cement dock to welcome her.

Libby's eyes were bright as she scanned Dunmore Town once more. She hugged her friend tightly, hardly able to believe that she was back on Harbour Island after all this time. It had been so long since she'd been in the Bahamas. Eight whole years.

Too long. Much too long.

She'd realised that the moment she'd set foot on the dock by the pastel pink Custom House. Her month of misgivings had vanished. Her weeks of worrying fled. All her 'what if's disappeared.

She hadn't wanted to come at all. When her mentor Professor Dietrich had announced her destination, she had balked.

'I've been there already,' she'd said stubbornly.

But he had just smiled. 'All the better, then. You'll have contacts.'

No amount of protesting could sway him, either. And now, for the first time, Libby was glad. She felt calm, sensible, adult. She realised now that she should have come back to this tiny Bahamian island years ago.

It would have been expensive, yes. But its cost in other than monetary terms had been dear as well. She should have faced the past, vanquished it, and moved on.

Well, better late than never, she told herself as she gave Maddy one last hug, then stepped back and turned to nod at the dark-haired boy of seven who was lying on his stomach behind her peering down into the water.

'I have someone I want you to meet, Maddy.' She beckoned to the boy who sprang to his feet and came to stand beside her. Libby laid her hand on his shoulder. 'I'd like you to meet my son, Maddy. This is Sam.'

If it had been possible for the ebony-skinned Maddy to have turned ashen, Libby thought she would have. The older woman's eyes grew wide and round, her jaw sagged. She looked for one long moment at the bony little boy and then her eyes turned to Libby; they spoke volumes.

Libby smiled ruefully, her hand tightened momentarily on Sam's shoulder and he wiggled away. 'I'm sorry,' she said to Maddy. 'I should've warned you. When I said I needed a house for two people, you probably thought I meant another researcher.'

'Don't know what I thought,' Maddy murmured, shaking Sam's hand, still looking as if she'd seen a ghost, 'but it weren't this. How you doin', honey?'

'I'm fine,' Sam said promptly and gave her a devastating, gap-toothed grin. 'I saw a crab down there. A big un.' He pointed to the clear turquoise water lapping the dock. 'Right out in the open.'

'You'll see lotsa 'em 'fore you go home, sweetie,' Maddy said. 'Oh, gracious,' she murmured. She took another long look, then gave him a smile, patted him on the head, and drew a shaky breath before she turned back to Libby. She shook her head and the look she gave Libby was sympathetic. 'Oh, my, oh, my.'

Libby felt a faint defensive bristling. She knew Maddy had guessed at once who Sam's father was. How could she not, after all?

Sam was a miniature Alec. They shared the same dark hair, the same strong features, the same intensity. In the boy one found a whirlwind. In the man, an elemental force.

Libby had long since come to terms with it. She saw Sam for himself now, not as Alec's son. But she knew what Maddy saw and what Maddy was thinking, and it irritated her. She didn't want anyone's pity. She had what she wanted—an education, a future, and Sam.

Once, years ago, it was true—she'd wanted Alec. But he hadn't wanted her. No, that wasn't quite true. He'd *wanted* her. He just hadn't loved her. And the moment that the beautiful Margo Hesse had come back into his life Libby had ceased to exist.

In less than two weeks, he had made Margo his wife.

At the time Libby had been devastated. She hadn't been able to understand how a man could make love to one woman and turn around and marry another.

But she was twenty-six years old now, no longer starry-eyed, and she had stopped wondering.

And, once she'd exorcised Alec's ghost this summer, she was getting married, too.

Michael had been asking her for almost a year. Until last month she'd said she wasn't ready, had too much to do, couldn't commit herself to any more.

'You take on new projects all the time,' Michael had argued.

'Not the same thing,' Libby replied.

But Michael was persistent. 'I love you.'

And she knew he did. He supported her desire to finish her master's. He took care of Sam when she had a class and her parents couldn't watch him. He was steady, reliable, dependable, and, Libby thought, he deserved a woman far better than she.

Michael disagreed. 'I love you,' he said again. 'Marry me.'

'I have to go to Harbour Island this summer,' Libby protested.

Michael smiled. 'Marry me when you get back.'

Libby paused, considering. It wasn't fair to Michael to keep him hanging on. Nor was it fair to Sam, or even to herself. She had to grow up, take charge of her life, make a decision. And there could be no better decision than Michael. He was everything that Alec was not.

'All right,' Libby said finally. 'Yes.'

And the minute she'd set foot on Bahamian soil again, she was sure she'd made the right choice. Looking around Dunmore Town, she saw it as she had seen it as a young woman of eighteen. She recognised it for the seductively tantalising place it was.

A small-town Iowa girl whose horizons, until then, had been Des Moines, Chicago, St Louis and St Paul, she'd been taken in by palm trees and turquoise seas, by the fragrance of pineapple and the sound of the waves. She'd been enchanted. By all that, and by Alec.

It was a fantasy world to a girl born and bred in the American midwest. What she and Alec had shared here was no more than that—a passing fancy, an infatuation.

He had been the hot-shot young actor-director, distraught and needing solace. She'd been the impressionable young nanny, ready to provide balm for his wounds.

She should have known it wouldn't last.

In turning away from her and going back to Margo, Alec was simply reverting to his true self. Eight years had gone by, and, unless Libby wanted the next eight or eighteen to be as barren as them, it was time she got on with her life.

Her summer on Harbour Island would do the trick, Libby thought. She looked forward to going home to Michael with a whole heart.

She smiled at Maddy now. 'It's so good to be back. I can hardly wait to see everyone. Is Lyman still fishing? Where's Sarah? Did Andrew go away to school in Nassau?'

Helping to stow two months' worth of luggage in the back of the Mitsubishi sedan, Maddy answered Libby's questions. 'Lyman goes out mos' days. He carries tourists along sometimes, gets fish for restaurants, too. Sarah, she got married to the Cash boy. Got a baby of her own now. And Andrew, he went to Nassau. But now he's gone to Florida State, you know.' Maddy beamed with pride at the accomplishments of her eldest son. 'Goin' to be a teacher, he says.'

Libby grinned, remembering the determined thirteen-year-old Andrew had been when she had been here last. 'It's good to have goals,' she said quietly. 'Sometimes they're all you've got.'

They were certainly all she'd had after Alec. They were all that had kept her going for the last eight years—her goals. And Sam.

She glanced at her son who was clambering into the back seat of Maddy's car. His dark eyes were wide, taking in everything. He'd been like a sponge since they'd got on the plane yesterday in Des Moines.

It had been his first trip on an aeroplane. He'd plied her with questions. More questions had come when they'd arrived last night in Nassau. Even more at the crack of dawn this morning when he'd insisted on walking on the beach and jumping into the ocean that, until yesterday, he'd never seen.

He wanted to see everything, do everything, under-stand everything. He was, indeed, Alec's son.

She got into the front seat next to Maddy. 'Where's the place you found for us?'

'Muellers' house. It's in town, not on the beach. Not so fancy as Bradens', you know.' Maddy gave a smiling shrug.

'I didn't expect it would be.' The Bradens were the family Libby had been nanny for that summer eight years before. Theirs had been a cedar and glass palace on the ocean side of the island.

A number of wealthy Americans and Europeans had holiday homes scattered about the hills above the three miles of almost deserted pink sand beach. Alec's parents had had a place there, too.

'Just two bedrooms,' Maddy told her, putting the car in gear. 'Small, small.'

'It'll be fine. Sam will be outside most of the time anyway. And I've got lots of work to do. I need to ask you the best people to talk to.'

'You jus' come to talk to people?' Maddy was amazed.

Libby nodded. That was the idea. She was to preserve as much of the oral history of the island as she could manage in eight weeks. At least that was her legitimate reason.

She looked around the palm-studded, pastel-painted hillside as Maddy's car bounced up the street from the dock. It was still beautiful, yes. Exotic. Tantalising.

But now she saw that the paint on the clapboard houses was peeling. The streets had pot-holes in them. Chickens ran loose on the roads.

She wasn't a starry-eyed child this time, an innocent fool. She would never again be taken in by a handsome man and a tinsel moon.

'I got to tell you somethin',' Maddy repeated as she turned the corner and pulled to a stop in front of a yellow frame house just visible behind a high board fence. She glanced over her shoulder at Sam who was asking,

'Is this it? Is this it?'

'Yes,' Libby said at Maddy's nod, and Sam shot out of the car to get a closer look. Maddy gave a grunt of satisfaction as he went.

Libby looked at her oddly.

Maddy sighed. 'Libby, you got to know.'

'So tell me, then,' Libby said, smiling. She opened the door and got out, impatient, too, wanting, as Sam did, to get on with settling in.

'Mr Alec...' Maddy said. 'He's back, too.'

Finding out she was pregnant had been no bigger shock. Libby stared, disbelieving. 'Alec? Here?'

No. He couldn't be.

'I was goin' to tell you anyways. I remembered 'bout you an' him, you see. But I didn't know 'bout...'bout the boy.'

No, she wouldn't have. Libby had left before she even knew it herself. She'd only sent Christmas cards to Maddy ever since—and she'd never said. What would have been the point?

She had tried to tell Alec. She'd written to him as soon as she'd found out. He was married already, of course, and that had made her hesitate. But in the end she'd tried because she thought he had a right to know.

He hadn't wanted to.

Her phone calls had met dead ends, and her letter had come back unopened in a larger envelope with a note attached in Alec's black scrawl. 'I'm married, Libby,' he had written. 'Forget me. You can be sure I'll forget you.'

*You can be sure I'll forget you.* Libby had shut her eyes against the pain of it. Well, you couldn't get much clearer than that. Face it, girl, she had told herself, you were a three-week stand. Margo was the real love of his life.

A few months later when she was standing in line in the supermarket, leafing through a gossip magazine, she had read that hot new film director Alec Blanchard and his actress wife, Margo Hesse, had a brand new daughter.

Hugely pregnant herself by this time, she had given a bitter laugh.

'Some stud, that Blanchard,' the woman standing in line behind her had commented.

'Too right,' Libby had muttered.

She had a fleeting moment's hope that that was why he'd married Margo, because he'd got her pregnant, too. Had he simply done the right thing? Libby wondered.

Who knew? Who cared? Even if he knew she was pregnant, he couldn't have married her, too.

He'd been dating Margo Hesse even before he'd come to Harbour Island. Libby had heard her name linked with his again and again. Margo had co-starred with him in the film he'd been making right before Libby had met him. Probably if she'd been there with him afterwards he'd never have turned to eighteen-year-old Libby for consolation when his stand-in had died.

But Margo hadn't been there. She hadn't come until later. And when she had, everything had changed.

Libby slapped the magazine back into the rack and said under her breath, 'You can be sure I'll forget you, too.'

The trouble was, she hadn't. Not completely. In some perverse way, every man she met, every man she dated— few though they were—she measured against those brief weeks of joy and love she'd shared with Alec.

Only with months and months of persistent wooing had Michael surmounted those memories, fitted himself in, become a necessary part of her life.

God bless Michael, Libby thought now.

'What you goin' to do?' Maddy asked her now, hoisting one of the suitcases and leading the way through the tall gate into the small overgrown yard.

There was nothing to do—not with regard to Alec anyway. With luck she could simply stay out of his way.

'What I've come here to do—work,' Libby said flatly, grabbing the other case and following. 'Alec doesn't matter. He has no part in my life.'

Maddy unlocked the door, then paused and looked back at Sam who was testing the strength of the bougainvillaea trellis. 'Does Mr Alec...know about...?'

'No.'

'He will.'

'That's his problem. He's married. He has a child of his own. More than one for all I know.'

He could have had a dozen for all she knew. She'd deliberately ignored anything else she might have seen or heard of Alec Blanchard over the years. It hadn't been easy. He was a household word now. Hollywood's main man.

'No, he jus' got the one.' Maddy carried the suitcase upstairs and into the larger of the two bedrooms and dropped it on the bed. 'She's here with him. Jus' him an' the little girl.'

'No Margo?'

Maddy stared at her. 'Margo, she's dead.'

'What?'

Maddy spread her hands. 'Car accident out in California. She an' some reporter fella goin' down to th'airport t'meet Mr Alec. Missed a curve, they say.' Maddy shook her head. 'Pity. Broke him up pretty bad, I reckon. You didn't hear?'

No, Libby hadn't heard. The beautiful, vibrant Margo Hesse dead? She sat down abruptly, her fingers clenching in her lap.

'Not surprised you ain't heard really,' Maddy went on. 'Mr Alec don't go for lots of publicity. He ain't one for stories in the papers, if he can help it.'

'Mmm.'

Maybe that was why Libby had been so successful at missing stories about him, she thought now. Maybe there had been little written. His films were, of course, legendary and well-reviewed. But his personal life seemed off limits. Little ever appeared about him and Margo and their daughter.

Margo, Libby remembered, had been an up-and-coming actress at the time he'd married her, a sultry blonde with a Marilyn Monroe pout. She didn't think, however, now that she reflected on it, that she remembered Margo being in another movie. Well, she hadn't had to work. Maybe she'd been satisfied as a devoted wife and mother.

'Poor Margo,' Libby said and then, remembering Sam and the strong bond she shared with her own child, she added, 'Her poor daughter.'

Maddy just nodded, not speaking, just took the clothes and tucked them away in drawers.

Libby did not say, 'Poor Alec.' She did not even think it. Not then. Not later. She had no emotions left for him at all.

She didn't see Alec, but she knew he was there. He was everywhere she went. How could he not be when all she had to do was walk down the street and people stopped what they were doing to glance at her?

She'd been here three days now, poking about the town, renewing acquaintances, making contacts. And, while she never mentioned Alec or Sam, she doubted that there was anyone on the island who hadn't heard. The island grapevine did its work well.

'Long time ago,' she heard them murmur. 'Her and Mr Alec. Only got to look at the boy.'

They were unfailingly polite to her, though. They smiled. Those who remembered her greeted her warmly, opened their arms to both her and Sam. She knew they understood. Children like Sam, born out of wedlock, were not that unusual on the island. More than one man had come and left a permanent reminder of himself.

But most of those men did not come back.

Alec had. Probably more than once. His family, after all, owned a home here. If anyone was the interloper, it was Libby, and she knew it.

She knew, too, that she should leave. Her mission was accomplished—the unspoken one, at least. It had taken her only moments to realise that she was no longer the foolish young woman who had fallen in love with Alec Blanchard. With joy she put Alec behind her now, made him part of her past. If she regretted the circumstances, she didn't regret Sam. But, regrets or not, she was ready to move on.

But for all that she, personally, was ready to go home, she couldn't leave without finishing her work.

She didn't want to think what Professor Dietrich would say if she went back to Iowa without the material she'd come for. He had been her mentor for seven long years. She owed him—and herself—its completion.

Besides, Sam didn't know any of her turmoil. These two months were a holiday for him, the first real vacation away from home he'd ever had.

She could hear him now, out in the road playing two square with several of the town kids. His laugh made her smile. His joy made her life complete. For Sam's pleasure and Dr Dietrich's satisfaction, she could live with the knowledge that Alec was only a mile away.

At least he was a mile away. With luck they would come no closer than that.

There was a brisk tap at the front door.

'Come on in,' Libby called, expecting Maddy with the day's catch of fish. She stood and scraped her papers into a pile on the desk, then turned, a smile of welcome on her face.

'Hello, Libby.' It was Alec.

Her smile faded, her stomach knotted. He hadn't changed. Not at all. Other men his age had begun to grow chunky. Their hair had started to thin, their eyes to tire. But Alec was the same as he'd always been—only more so.

The lean whipcord strength she remembered seemed all too evident, contained in a mere T-shirt and cotton trousers. His dark hair was wind-ruffled and wanted cutting. His face was taut, the skin tight over the bones. It took only a glance to confirm that he was every bit as handsome and compelling as he had ever been.

Her fingers found purchase on the back of the chair, tightening reflexively. She drew a slow, steadying breath.

'Alec,' she acknowledged coldly when she could speak. 'What do you want?'

'I heard you were here,' he said in the same voice that had once sent shivers of love and longing down her spine. 'I wanted to see you.'

Libby met his gaze evenly. 'Why?'

'Because we were friends.'

'Is that what we were?' Libby asked bitterly.

His smile was grim. 'Not exactly thrilled to see me, are you?'

'Should I be?'

He sighed. 'No,' he said after a moment. 'Probably not. But I knew we'd run into each other sooner or later. I just thought I'd rather pick the time and place.'

'If you'd keep to your own side of the island,' Libby said rudely, 'it needn't have happened at all.'

Her vehemence seemed to surprise him. 'I wanted it to,' he said again.

'All right,' she said shortly. 'You've seen me. Go home.'

Alec shook his head. 'I don't think so.'

'Alec——'

'We have a lot to talk about.' He still stood in the middle of the room, shrinking it, his eyes on her, making her squirm.

She wished, if they'd had to meet, they had met at the dock or on the beach—anywhere outside where Alec Blanchard didn't take up all the available space.

'No, we don't,' Libby said and looked pointedly at the door.

Alec didn't move, just waited.

She sighed, knowing he wouldn't leave until he'd said whatever it was he'd come to say. They might as well get it over with. 'OK. Talk. Sit down if you must,' she added ungraciously as she went to stand behind the dining-table.

'You used to be more welcoming.'

'Surprise, surprise.'

He scowled, but took a seat on the couch, crossing one leg over the other knee. He wore a pair of faded blue trousers and the fabric pulled across his thighs, outlining the muscles beneath. Libby remembered the strength of those thighs, the power of the man. Her face burned. Desperately she shoved herself away from the table.

'How about some iced tea?' she asked, needing some herself to quench the sudden fire she felt.

'Sounds good.'

She had hoped for a momentary respite in the kitchen, but Alec followed her in, lounging against the door-jamb, his eyes never leaving her. There was a hunger in them that was all too familiar. Libby looked away, opening the refrigerator.

'Why did you come, Alec? What do you want?'

'To see you. To catch up. You were a kid the last time I saw you.'

'A kid?' Her voice was scornful, but his words hurt.

'A beautiful child.' The tone in which he said the words made her knees weak.

'That you took advantage of,' Libby bit out.

His mouth twisted. 'Maybe I did,' he allowed.

She whirled and glared at him. 'Is that why you're back now? Do you want more? Because if you do, you're sure as hell not getting it!'

He grinned. 'The kitten's developed claws.'

'I'm not a kitten. I never was. I'm a woman, Alec.' She turned away and concentrated on dropping ice cubes into tall glasses, then filled them up.

'I've noticed,' Alec said drily.

'Don't bother.' She handed him a glass, careful not to touch him, then led the way back into the living-room, seating herself in the high-backed chair closest to the window.

For a long moment neither of them spoke. Then Alec said conversationally, 'They say you're on the island doing a study.'

Libby nodded. 'That's right. Oral history.'

Alec smiled, as if her choice amused him, then settled on to the couch. 'Do you like it?'

'Yes.'

'That's what you wanted to do.'

'Yes.'

'You were serious, then, about your goals?' He was looking at her intently, as though it mattered.

To her it had. Eight years ago they had lain on the beach together, their bodies touching, their breath mingling, their dreams shared. And while Alec had told her about his first film, just finished, about the pains and joys of that experience and about his hopes and dreams for a successful directing career, Libby had told him how she would be the first of her family to enrol in college.

She had told him how excited they all were, how determined she was. It might have sounded like small potatoes to someone like him, but she had meant it.

'I'm going to make them proud of me,' she'd vowed with the enthusiasm of youth.

And Alec had said, 'Good for you. You can do it.'

Of course, it hadn't happened the way she'd envisaged it. It had been a longer, harder road because of Sam. But, after a fashion, with a few major obstacles surmounted, she had done what she'd said she would do. And her family was proud of her. She was proud of herself.

'I was completely serious,' she said now, deliberately meeting his gaze.

He nodded and took a long swallow of the tea. 'That's good. I'm glad. You must be serious if you're still going strong eight years later. What're you working on, a PhD?'

'My master's.'

He looked surprised. 'That's all?'

She shrugged. 'I dropped out for a while.'

'Dropped out? But you were so gung-ho. Why'd you quit?'

'I had another commitment that was more important.'

'What commitment?' He was frowning now, challenging her, as if asking what could have been more vital than the degree she'd been so determined to get.

Far out in the harbour Libby could hear the persistent buzz of an outboard motor. Beyond the gate came the laughter of playing children. Just outside the window, crickets chirped and birds twittered.

She lifted her chin and looked straight at him, wondering if even the truth would shatter his complacency. 'I had your son.'

For an eternity Alec didn't move.

She might have wondered if he'd even heard her, but she saw the colour drain from his face.

So, she thought. It was possible to rattle him. But it was a hollow sort of satisfaction.

Still, she wasn't going to lie to him. She never had. She wouldn't start now. Not to protect either herself or him.

He was still staring at her. 'My son? You had my son? You got pregnant, Lib?' His voice cracked. He was as white as the coconut meat Libby helped Maddy to grate.

In answer Libby got to her feet and walked to the window, pulling aside the curtain to look past the fence towards the street. 'Your son,' she said and nodded.

Alec hauled himself up from the couch and came to stand beside her. She pointed. His gaze followed the movement of her hand.

There were half a dozen children playing in the dusty street. Only one of the six was white. He had unruly dark hair that flopped across his forehead, long skinny legs and dirty bare feet. He laughed just then and Alec could see that one of his top front teeth was missing.

'My God.'

His fingers caught Libby's wrist and gripped it tight. His gaze swivelled, fastening on hers. '*Why...?* For pity's sake, Libby, why didn't...why didn't you tell me?'

She heard rage and pain and every emotion she'd ever hoped to hear in his voice. But it was too late. Eight years too late.

She pulled her arm away. 'I called. No one would let me talk to you. You were married, remember? They were protecting that.' Her mouth twisted at the memory of the run-around she'd been given by all those many well-meaning people. 'I understood. Margo got there first, after all,' she added with an ironic smile.

'Margo——'

'But I did try. I thought maybe you'd want to know.'

'To know?' He looked at her, aghast. 'Just to know? That you were having my son?'

Libby gave a bitter laugh. 'What else? You could hardly marry me. You already had one pregnant wife. What did you need with another?'

He looked stricken. 'You should have told Harve.'

Libby shook her head. There was no way Libby could have told Alec's secretary-cum-assistant. Harve Milliken's job was to protect Alec from groupies and hangers-on. And from the first time he'd met her, he'd lumped Libby into that category, never seeing in her what Alec had.

Harve had wanted the best for his boss. The best, in Harve's eyes, had never been Libby Portman.

'Harve wasn't the father of my baby.'

'For goodness sake, Libby...' he raked his hands through his hair '...you must have needed help...money...'

'I didn't want money,' she said. 'I wasn't asking for that. I just thought you should know.' She shrugged and walked away from the window. 'When they wouldn't let me talk to you, I wrote.' She spread her hands.

Alec stared at her. 'The letter? *That* was what you were writing to me about?' His face was still white. She could see the pulse ticking furiously in his temple. He swallowed hard. His gaze went again to the boy in the street, then came back once more to Libby.

'Yes. I certainly wasn't trying to get you!'

He shut his eyes. 'Oh, lord.' He looked almost ill.

The gate clicked just then and Maddy came into the garden, a shopping-bag in her arms. She came up the steps and, with a light tap, opened the door.

Her eyes went from Libby to Alec and back again. 'Oh, my.'

'Hi, Maddy. Did you bring us some fish?' Libby mustered her most matter-of-fact voice.

Maddy licked her lips, then rummaged in the shopping-bag and slapped a packet on the table. 'That

I did. Plenty for tonight and tomorrow too. How you been, Mr Alec?'. she added, giving him a surreptitious glance.

Alec shook his head. He backed towards the door. 'I need to think,' he mumbled.

His eye caught Libby's for just a moment, then slid away. 'I . . . have to go. I'll talk to you, Libby.'

'He knows,' Maddy said into the silence he left behind.

'Yes,' Libby agreed. 'Now he knows.'

# CHAPTER TWO

'YOU sick or something, Mom?' Sam asked.

Libby shook her head as she concentrated on washing the dinner dishes later that evening. 'I'm fine.'

'You're awful quiet.'

Libby laughed. 'You're just not used to the lack of noise around here. No television. No radio. No telephone.'

Sam shrugged. 'Maybe. But last night you talked to me.'

And tonight she'd scarcely said a word. She had begun to understand the implications of Alec's knowing. She'd been preoccupied with his arrival and with everything that had passed between them all through dinner, but she didn't think that Sam had noticed. Now guiltily she made an effort to focus on him. 'So what did you do today?'

'Went swimming with Arthur down by the dock. An' then we fed Lulu at the cricket grounds.'

Arthur was Maddy's youngest. Lulu was the island horse. Her function in life seemed to be keeping the weeds down on the scraggly patch of grass known as the Royal Cricket Grounds and, periodically, giving rides to the island's children.

It hadn't taken Sam long to make friends with either Arthur or Lulu.

Libby watched him now, drying the dishes with more vigour than ability. There was an eager light in his eyes. This trip had been good for him, broadening his horizons, opening his eyes to a world larger than the one he lived in back home in Iowa.

Despite Alec, she couldn't be sorry they had come.

'So can we?' Sam asked.

Libby blinked, coming back to reality. 'Can we what, sweetie?'

'Go to the beach? Arthur says it's super. Better'n the harbour. Waves 'n' reefs. Can we, huh?'

Libby pulled the plug and let the water pour noisily down the drain. She'd been avoiding the beach. It held too many memories. But she couldn't be plagued by more than had already been today. If she had to go, now was the time. 'Why not?'

She took a beach towel to sit on and a flashlight in case darkness fell before they got back. The sun was behind them, low in the sky, and when they reached the rise of the hill the breeze off the ocean picked up, cooling her cheeks as she walked. The pavement was still warm through the thin soles of her sandals, and she walked at first reluctantly, then more rapidly as if pulled, drawn like the tide to the shore.

Eight years ago this beach, these three miles of pink coral sand, had been her second home. Every day she'd taken Tony and Alicia Braden, aged eight and ten, there to swim and to play in the sand. And at night, when Tony and Alicia had gone to bed, she'd taken a flashlight and walked back down to dream her impossible dreams as she'd dug her toes in the soft wet sand.

They had been nights just like this one with the sun going down behind her. And she would come down and stare out at the ocean, thinking that if she, Elizabeth Mary Portman, an eighteen-year-old land-locked Iowan, could wind up on the most beautiful beach in the Caribbean for a whole summer, then anything—anything at all—could happen.

And when she had met Alec, it had.

But she wouldn't let herself think about that now. Alec was too close to her tonight. Too immediate. Too real.

Forget him, she told herself fiercely and forced herself to focus on Sam as he skipped down the path to the ocean, shouting at her to come, to hurry, to see what he had found.

It was Sam who mattered now, not Alec. Sam. And when she got home, Michael. Alec was her past. Sam and Michael were her future.

'Come on, Mom,' Sam shouted again.

Libby slipped off her sandals and ran after him.

Sam found a Coke can from the Netherlands, an empty tube of sun-screen from Poland, a water-bottle from France. Libby, despite her best intentions, found memories of the past.

Sam raced in and out of the incoming tide, dug trenches, built castles, turned cartwheels in the sand.

Libby spread out her towel, wrapped her arms around her knees and watched.

But what she saw was not Sam, but Tony and Alicia Braden, her charges of that summer eight long years ago.

What she felt was not a detached anthropological interest in the shipboard flotsam and jetsam that Sam laid before her, but the remembered awe and starry-eyed amazement of a sheltered young woman come for the first time to a foreign land.

'Watch me!' Sam yelled, leaping into the ocean, jumping the waves. 'Watch me, Mom!'

And Libby watched. But it was Tony she was seeing in her mind's eye as he had leaped in and out of the surf all those years before.

It was a day that, no matter how much she might like to, she knew she would never forget...

* * *

It had been a long day, a tiring one. Alicia had been cranky, Tony had lost a tooth. Neither had been happy when their parents had informed them they wouldn't be home that evening, that their neighbours, the Blanchards, had invited them over for cocktails and dinner instead.

'Can we come?' Tony demanded.

'Not this time,' his father said.

'You promised you'd play cards with me,' Alicia fussed. 'And Mama was going to cut out the Roaring Twenties paper dolls.'

'In the morning,' Mrs Braden promised. 'It's important that we go tonight, lovely. It's a party for Alec.'

Tony's eyes widened. 'He's back? Really? Truly?'

'Just for a while,' his mother said, then turned to Libby and explained, 'Our neighbours' son is Alec Blanchard. You may have heard of him.'

'Yes.' Even provincial midwestern Libby had heard of Alec Blanchard. An actor of brooding intensity and considerable fame, Alec Blanchard was becoming a household word. Just last month in a weekly news magazine Libby had read about his new film.

He had tried his hand at directing this film as well as acting in it. The writer of the article had waxed lyrical about his talent, had spoken of the sparks that flew between him and his co-star Margo Hesse, and about how well he'd borne the stress of something or other; Libby didn't remember what.

Evelyn Braden did.

'Such a shame what happened. Poor Alec. He's taking a bit of time off,' Mrs Braden said to Libby as she played gin rummy with Alicia. 'It's been a hard year for him, what with the film, Margo's temperament and then Clive Gilbert getting killed.'

Libby looked blank, not knowing who Clive Gilbert was.

Her confusion must have showed on her face for Mrs Braden went on, 'Clive was Alec's stunt man. His double, you know. Alec did most of his own work. But his contract prevented him from doing the riskiest bits. Clive did those. He was killed last month in Spain. Trampled by a horse doing a re-shoot of a scene. He was, perhaps, Alec's best friend as well. Alec's taken it very hard.'

Libby supposed that anyone with an ounce of sensitivity would. Intellectually you might be able to say that Clive Gilbert had died doing his job, but emotionally it would be like having someone die in your stead. She shuddered at the thought.

'And Margo has been no help at all. She hasn't even been around. Took herself off right after the funeral. So sensitive, everyone said.' Mrs Braden clucked her disapproval. 'Anyway, Alec's come to his folks' for some well deserved rest and relaxation, and Catherine—that's his mother—is determined to cheer him up, so she's having a few people over. Life does go on, you know.'

'Yes,' Libby agreed, with all the naïveté of eighteen years.

Evelyn Braden smiled. 'So, if you could take the kids to the beach for an evening picnic while we're gone, it would be greatly appreciated.'

So she did. And after she and the children had eaten the picnic supper that Maddy had packed for them, Libby sat on a towel watching Alicia build a sand-castle and Tony snorkel inside the reef.

Every once in a while, when the wind shifted, she could hear the sounds of laughter from beyond the thick banks of shrubs that rose up the hill behind the beach.

Life did, it seemed, go on. And, Libby thought, it sounded as if Alec Blanchard and company were enjoying it.

Let them. Libby didn't need a party or booze or any of the things the Alec Blanchards of the world required. She had the sand and the surf and the setting sun. She, who had detassled corn, picked beans and mucked out hog barns, was having a summer she would never forget as long as she lived. She lay back and closed her eyes, content.

A shadow fell, blocking out the sun.

A spattering of water dropped on her. Her eyes snapped open, expecting to see a squall moving in.

She saw a man standing over her, dripping wet.

'Hello.'

His voice was rough and warm, slightly smoky. It reminded Libby of the sip of brandy David Braden had permitted her after dinner the night before.

She stared, then swallowed. 'H-hello.'

He was not the sort of man to whom she was accustomed to speaking. Even in her new, glitzy summer lifestyle, men like this—lean, dark, handsome men who made her pulses flutter and her palms damp—were few and far between.

She glanced around wildly, wondering where Tony and Alicia had got to. A wave of relief washed over her when she spotted them dashing in and out of the waves down the beach.

'Tony! Lisha! Come on back!' she called at once, anxious to establish the fact that she wasn't alone.

The man glanced in the direction of the children, then turned back to her. He grinned. 'Calling in the reinforcements?'

Libby coloured, abashed at how transparent her motive must have seemed. But heaven knew she would need reinforcements, unless he was planning on simply passing by.

That he wasn't became immediately obvious. He sat down on the sand next to her towel, and when the children ran up seconds later he had a grin for them, too. 'Hi, Tony, Hi, Lisha.'

Both children stopped dead.

Then, 'Alec!' Alicia shrieked and flung her arms around him.

Tony let out a whoop. 'Alec! They said you were here!'

Libby stared. Alec? Alec Blanchard? This man was Alec Blanchard, famous actor, household word? She wondered that she hadn't recognised him, then realised that she'd never seen him in a movie dripping wet.

But if he was *the* Alec Blanchard, the man for whom the party was being held right up the hill, what was he doing here?

She opened her mouth to ask when a lilting female voice called, 'Yoohoo, Alec?' from somewhere up beyond the trees.

The man sitting next to her groaned. He glanced around almost desperately, then held out his hand to Tony. 'Lend me your snorkel.' He looked at the three of them. 'You haven't seen me,' he said. Without waiting for a confirmation of his blatant lie, he strode towards the water and dived beneath the surf.

Libby stared at the spot where he'd disappeared, but the waves broke over it, and if the tip of the snorkel was visible, it wasn't by much.

Moments later a diminutive dark-haired woman and a tall twentyish blonde appeared where the path opened on to the beach. The older dark-haired woman scanned the beach, her hands on her hips, her expression grim. The blonde headed right for Libby and the children.

'I'm looking for Alec Blanchard. Have you seen him?'

Tony and Alicia looked at Libby, tight-lipped, wide-eyed. And Libby, who'd never told a lie in her life, looked right at the woman and said, 'No, ma'am.'

'You do know who he is?'

'Yes, ma'am,' Libby said dutifully.

The woman sighed again, this time, Libby suspected, as much at her apparent lack of wit as at Alec's disappearance. 'Well, if you do see him, tell him...' She broke off and ran a hand through stylishly windswept hair. 'Never mind,' she said. 'He knows.'

Turning on her heel, she walked back up the beach to join the older woman. 'Apparently he hasn't been here, Catherine.'

Alec's mother, Libby decided, remembering that Catherine was what Mrs Braden had called her. She had the same dark good looks, too. She looked worried now, not annoyed as the blonde did.

'Poor Alec,' Libby heard her say. She gave Libby a fleeting smile which made her feel guilty for the deception, then the two of them picked their way through the sand spurs back up the path from the beach.

Libby watched them go, curious. Why was Alec Blanchard avoiding them? Why was he avoiding a party given in his honour?

She looked back out at the ocean. A sleek dark head bobbed to the surface momentarily, then disappeared again.

'We should be going,' she said to Tony and Alicia.

'Can't,' Tony said. 'I gotta get my snorkel.'

'He'll get it back to you,' Libby promised.

'I want to wait.'

In fact, Libby did, too. She wanted to know more about this man she had just lied for, wanted to feel again the shiver of awareness, the fundamental attraction that had jolted her the moment her eyes met his.

'Just a few minutes, then,' she agreed. So she sat back down on the beach in the deepening twilight, building a sand-castle with Alicia and Tony, ignoring the bursts of laughter and gaiety from the party still going on; ignoring, too, the periodic appearances of the blonde woman when she came down to scan the beach. And she determinedly paid no attention at all to the occasional appearance of Alec's sleek dark head above the waves.

At last it was too dark to wait any longer. He showed no signs of coming ashore, and Libby realised that he was probably going to wait until they left as well. To be sure, it would save him from having to answer a myriad questions from Alicia and Tony.

'Come on,' Libby said finally. 'We're going.' She picked up her towel, got Tony and Alicia to gather the picnic things, and herded them, still protesting, up the beach.

The twilight seemed to vanish as Libby picked her way up the path to Bradens' house.

'Slow down,' she called to Tony who was bounding on ahead with the only light in the jungly blackness. The beam bobbed and swayed as he skipped up the path and around the bend of the mangroves with Alicia following him.

'Tony!' Libby, the towel slung around her shoulders, the picnic basket banging against her knees, tripped and would have fallen if a pair of strong hands hadn't reached from behind just then and grabbed her.

A shriek started from her lips, only to be smothered with a kiss. It was a brief kiss, lasting just long enough to shift the axis of her world.

'Shh,' a voice said against her mouth, and she would have recognised that smoky sound anywhere. 'It's just me.'

Alec.

'And I didn't go to all that trouble to avoid them, just to have you let them know where I am now, did I?'

Numbly, Libby shook her head, her heart going double time, bells ringing in her head. He'd kissed her! Alec Blanchard had kissed her.

Even now he was still holding her arms, his hands cool and damp against her overheated skin. Her lips tingled. Her mind spun. That kiss! Had it been just to shut her up or...?

But she couldn't even form the thought in her mind.

'S-sorry,' she spluttered and expected him to let go of her then, but he didn't. One hand dropped away and took the picnic basket out of her grasp, but the other slid down her arm and she felt his fingers lock firmly with hers.

'Come on. Let's catch up with the kids.' Then he towed her, dazed and disbelieving, up the path through the woods.

Tony and Alicia were waiting on the porch.

'I knew you'd bring it,' Tony said, taking the snorkel from him, while Libby fumbled in her beach-bag for the house key. When she finally found it, her nerveless fingers dropped it, and she watched, mortified, as Alec bent to scoop it up.

'Allow me.' Unlocking the door, he pushed it open, then stepped back as Libby and the children entered.

Libby, still flustered from the memory of his mouth on hers, slanted him a quick glance as she passed. He winked. Her face flamed.

'Just put the picnic things in the kitchen,' she mumbled. 'Thank you for carrying it back. Excuse me now. I have to get the kids ready for bed.'

'But——' Tony protested.

'Alec's here. We have to——' Alicia began.

'Baths. And then bed,' Libby insisted with all the authority she could muster. 'It's late.'

Shooing Tony and Alicia ahead of her, she fled upstairs, praying that the man who unnerved her so would be gone by the time she came back.

She got the children through baths in record time and, while they were getting into pyjamas, she grabbed a quick shower herself. Tony wanted to come down and say goodnight to Alec. Alicia wanted him to read them a bedtime story. Libby said a firm no to both.

'I'm sure he's gone back to his party.'

'I don't think he wanted to be at his party,' Tony said frankly.

'He's too much of a gentleman to stay away the whole time,' Libby replied. 'He probably just needed a break. Now brush your teeth and scoot on to bed.'

Alicia tugged on her arm. 'Read to us?'

Libby sighed. She wanted nothing more than to go downstairs into the privacy of the living-room, where she could run the amazing events of the evening over in her mind. But she wasn't here to daydream. She read them a chapter of their current book, then kissed them both and put out the light. Then, breathing a sigh of relief, touching her still tingling lips with her fingers, she pulled the door shut and tiptoed down the steps.

Alec was leaning against the wall. Still sandy, still wearing only a pair of swimming trunks, he smiled up at her. 'At last.'

Libby stopped stock still and stared. He was, she was quite certain now, the most attractive man she'd ever seen. His sheer masculine power rendered her mute, and she might have stood there forever if his grin hadn't widened.

'Taking root, are you?' he teased.

Face flaming, she licked her lips and slowly came the rest of the way down. 'I—I thought you'd left. What about your party?'

'They aren't missing me.'

'They came looking.'

'That was two hours ago when they were feeling like good Samaritans. By now I'm sure they're feeling no pain.' There was a wry weariness in his tone that made her take a closer look at him.

He had shaken her to the foundation of her being when he had kissed her, but she thought now that he looked shaken himself. There was a haunted look in his dark eyes that she didn't imagine was normal for Alec Blanchard. And she doubted it was the kiss that had rattled him, but something far more earth-shattering. She remembered Clive Gilbert.

'You are,' she said softly. 'In pain, I mean.'

Alec's eyes narrowed and he looked at her sharply.

Libby stood her ground, unflinching under his gaze.

He sighed. 'Bright girl,' he said. 'Perceptive.'

Libby shrugged self-consciously. She'd had only to look at him to realise that what Mrs Braden had said was true: Alec Blanchard was suffering.

And however much his parents might have tried to distract him, a party was not the solace he was looking for.

'Would you like some coffee or something? I mean, if you're going to stay?'

He smiled. 'Thanks. Coffee.'

She started towards the kitchen, then turned back. 'If you're going to...hang around, you—er—might want a shower. And Mr Braden probably has some clothes you could wear.'

Alec just looked at her for a moment. Then he smiled. It was a smile that melted her. 'Right,' he said softly and padded towards the bathroom.

While Alec showered Libby fetched a pair of shorts and a T-shirt from David Braden's wardrobe, telling herself that what she was doing was perfectly all right, that Alec was a friend of the Bradens, that they would approve.

But she knew she really didn't care whether they approved or not.

Good or bad, right or wrong; suddenly it didn't mean anything to her. She had sensed a need in Alec Blanchard, and she was filling it. She was operating on another plane of reality altogether.

She set the clothes just inside the door of the steamy bathroom and shut it again quickly, not permitting herself even a glimpse of the naked male form behind the shower door. Then, hands clammy, pulse pounding, she went out to the kitchen to make the coffee and, while she was there, poured herself a tall glass of iced tea.

She was drinking it rapidly when Alec reappeared. He was barefoot, his hair tousled and damp. David Braden's shirts and shorts were much too big for Alec. But in spite of the ill-fitting clothes he looked wonderful to Libby.

'Much better,' Alec said, smiling a devastating smile and combing his hair with his fingers.

Libby swallowed. 'C-coffee's ready.'

He took the cup from her, sipped it, then regarded her solemnly over the top. His eyes were dark and knowing, the sort of eyes that could see to the bottom of your soul, Libby thought. Her own eyes fluttered away.

'So you're the summer girl,' he said.

Libby blinked. 'What? Oh, you mean the nanny? Yes.' She hadn't heard the term before, but it fitted. She felt so different here from the way she did back home, almost as if she were two different girls, had two different existences—a summer life and a regular one. Especially tonight.

'You like it here?' he asked her.

She nodded quickly. 'Oh, yes. It's so...new. So different.'

'From where?'

'Iowa.'

Alec smiled. 'Should have been Kansas.'

'Why?'

'You look like the sort who'd have a dog named Toto and an Auntie Em.'

Libby felt her cheeks burn. 'A hayseed, in other words.' What had she expected? That he'd find her attractive? A worldly man like Alec Blanchard?

But Alec shook his head. 'Not a hayseed. An innocent. You look pure, undefiled.'

Now Libby's cheeks were positively aflame. 'I suppose you think that's a compliment?' she said archly.

He nodded. 'I do.'

But it didn't feel that way to Libby. It felt rather as if she'd been tried and found wanting. He could at least have thought she looked a bit worldly, even if she wasn't!

'Let's go out on the deck,' he said, and reached over to flick off the light. Still mortified, Libby stayed where she was until a strong hand reached back and snagged hers, towing her in his wake.

Alec dropped her hand when they were outside, leaning against the railing, staring out into the darkness. The moon behind him caught his profile in silhouette, outlining the strong nose, the determined chin, the lips that had—so briefly—touched hers.

'I owe you one, summer girl,' he said quietly.

Libby looked at him, confused. 'One what?'

'A thank you, I guess. For hiding me. I didn't need fun and games tonight. I appreciate it.'

Libby shrugged. 'I'm glad. Those ladies didn't.'

He grimaced. 'I know.'

'Was one of them your mother?'

'Yeah.'

'She looked worried.'

'She is worried. Thinks I should smile more, cheer up. "Put on a happy face."' His voice was bitter as he echoed her words.

Libby debated how to reply to that. Good sense told her just to nod, not to let on that she knew what he meant. But he was *hurting*. She could see it. And Libby didn't like people to suffer pain. Throwing caution to the winds, she plunged in.

'I—I heard about...about Clive Gilbert,' she said in a low tone, one that he could ignore if he chose. 'I'm sorry.'

He didn't ignore it. He turned his head and looked at her. 'Sorry?' His tone was even more bitter. 'Yeah, me too. I'm sorry as hell. But it doesn't bring Clive back, does it?'

He was almost glaring at her, daring her to minimise his pain. She couldn't see so much as feel the intensity of his gaze. They were so close that the heat from his body warmed hers. But it wasn't the heat so much as the pain that she wanted to share.

Instinctively she reached out and touched his cheek. 'No,' she said. 'No. Nothing will bring him back.'

She expected that he would jerk away or bat her hand down. But he didn't move, and she felt his cheek, cool and rough beneath her palm.

From down along the beach came the sound of waves rushing along the sand. From far overhead Libby heard the hum of a propeller engine. From out of the darkness came the croak of a frog, the hum of a hundred insects. But louder than all of them was the thrum of the blood in her head.

Then Alec muttered, 'Oh, lord,' and reached for her, hauling her into his arms.

This kiss wasn't brief; it wasn't grateful. It was hungry, desperate, needy. It asked for things that Libby didn't even know she had to give. But she didn't say no.

Alec's lips were as warm as his skin was cool. They brought her to life, opened vistas to her she'd never imagined. His hands moulded her body against his, letting her feel the surge of arousal in him. His hips pressed into hers, his mouth locked with hers, his hands slid under her shirt, seeking her breasts, finding them.

Libby whimpered, her own need astonishing her, filling her, and instinctively she leaned into him. It felt so good, so right to comfort him.

And then, quite suddenly, Alec pulled back.

Not far. Just enough so that the cool night air slipped between their heated bodies. Just far enough so she could hear the desperate rasp of his breathing.

And in it she could still hear his pain. She touched him again, her fingers caressing his neck, and this time he did flinch.

'Don't!' But his voice held more desperation than anger. 'Don't let me.'

'Let you?' Libby wasn't sure what he meant.

He gave a harsh laugh. 'Ah, innocence. See, I told you.' He lifted his head and looked at her. 'Would you really have given yourself to me, summer girl? Would you do that to help me forget?'

Would she?

Libby's face burned at the thought, and even more at the very real possibility that she might.

She'd never felt this way before, had never been so caught up in a man, in a given moment, that all else seemed to fade away. No man had ever touched her this way before. She'd never felt such desire, such hunger. She'd certainly never responded like this. It hadn't been comfort at all, not when she stepped back to look at it.

She felt the merest child, foolish, naïve—everything he'd said she was.

'I...' She shook her head, looking down, unable to face him, drowning in emotions she hadn't even known she was capable of.

And Alec's hand came up and stroked through her long flyaway hair. His fingers were gentle now; trembling, she thought. They touched her chin, lifting it so that she looked up at him. And then, against the moonlight, she saw his cheek curve as he smiled at her. It was a warm smile, a tender, loving one.

Libby smiled back, and it was as if the world had shrunk until it contained nothing but the two of them.

'What's your name?'

'Libby.'

'Mom! I'm freezin'!' Sam, teeth chattering and goosepimpled, appeared suddenly in the falling darkness. Libby blinked.

'Oh, Sam. Oh, good heavens!' She got quickly to her feet, feeling guilty and not a little foolish at the warm flush that still tingled on her cheeks.

She wrapped her towel around Sam's shivering shoulders and rubbed him briskly. 'Come on.' She began to walk along the beach towards the path that led to town. Abruptly she stopped.

Far off near the point, in the very direction they were heading, she saw a dark-haired man and a small blonde girl heading their way.

'Who's that?' Sam asked, following her gaze.

But Libby didn't answer. There was a limit to how much she could take of Alec, past and present, in one night. She turned abruptly and made for the path near the hotel instead.

'Come along, Sam,' she said. 'It's getting late.'

\*   \*   \*

The clear light of day restored her equilibrium. Life went on, just as Evelyn Braden had said it did all those years ago.'

And even though she'd tossed and turned most of the night, Libby knew with certainty that nothing had changed.

She had seen Alec again. She had relived, for the first time in years, the night of their first meeting. But after the meeting, after the reminiscences, she was still twenty-six years old, still the mother of a seven-year-old boy, still a graduate student with a job to do and only seven and a half weeks now to do it in.

She got to work.

School, which had ended in their small Iowa city the last week in May, was still in session on Harbour Island. Libby considered the alternatives, allowed Sam a taste of three days without playmates, then, bright and early the morning after she'd seen Alec again, she enrolled him in school.

Sam didn't complain. 'Arthur will be there,' he said, eyes shining with anticipation.

And when Libby went off to do her interviews, she walked with him as far as the school.

Libby found herself glancing around, half expecting to see Alec lurking about somewhere. She was pleased that he wasn't.

'I'll meet you after,' she promised and dropped a kiss on the top of his head. 'We'll walk home together.'

''K. See you. There's Arthur.' And Sam took off, running into the dusty schoolyard.

Libby watched him go, glad now that she hadn't answered his question last night about who that man was, glad that Sam knew little and cared less about his father.

In the course of seven years he'd only asked a few questions about the man who'd sired him. When he was three, Sam had looked up from his trucks and said, 'Toby has a dad, and Jeremy has a dad. Where's my dad?'

And Libby had said, 'Your dad lives far away.'

'Can I see him?' Sam asked.

'No.'

Sam had waited to see if she might elaborate, but when she didn't, he'd shrugged with a three-year-old's equanimity and had gone back to driving his trucks.

Partly, Libby supposed, it was because his life wasn't really lacking in adult men. Her own father was around all the time. Once he'd got over his shock at Libby's pregnancy, Samuel Portman has been wonderfully supportive. Now 'Pop' doted on young Sam.

Her brothers, Jeff and Greg, were in high-school when Sam was born and for years had been more like older brothers than uncles to the little boy.

Not until this spring, when the Cub Scouts had a father-son banquet, had the question come up again.

'Pop will go with you,' Libby had said when Sam came home with the announcement.

'Couldn't you maybe call my father and ask him?' Sam had suggested.

For a split second Libby had wondered what would happen if she did. A tiny part of her would have loved to rock Alec Blanchard's boat.

But the momentary satisfaction she'd get would scarcely balance the chaos that would inevitably follow. Even if she could have got hold of Alec, she would never have done it. Not to herself nor to him. Nor especially to Sam.

'Sorry, love,' she'd said. 'Can't. Anyway, you know Pop loves Kentucky Fried Chicken. He'd be crushed if you didn't take him.'

Sam giggled because it was true.

That day was the last time either of them had mentioned Sam's father.

No one else spoke of him, either. Not even when Libby had told her family where she and Sam were spending the summer.

But after Sam had gone to bed that night, her mother had looked up from the mending. 'Do you think it's wise, Libby? Going back? Dredging it up again? After all, you have Michael now.'

But her father had said, 'Best thing she could do, get it out of her system. Good for you, Lib,' he'd said to her. 'Be done with it once and for all.'

And Libby, meeting his gaze, knew that all those years of careful silence hadn't fooled Samuel Portman.

They were alike in that way—needing to finish things, needing to get matters settled. He knew she'd never forgotten, knew she never would—unless she went back and made peace with herself.

Until last night she'd thought she was convinced she had.

Now she didn't know.

She had hoped her feelings for Alec would be dead and buried. They weren't. He angered her, which was only to be expected. But he made her heart beat faster, too.

'Passion,' she mocked herself. 'Worthless, foolish passion. That and nothing more.'

But she wished desperately that that urge for passion weren't there.

She hated herself for spending so much time thinking about him. Chances were he wasn't thinking about her.

Finally she had to force herself to concentrate on something else and as soon as she took Sam to school she went off in search of the fishermen she intended to interview.

She spent the morning talking to three old fishermen, taking notes frantically and using up three whole tapes. She got absorbed in her work, felt the satisfaction of accomplishing something, and went home for lunch well pleased.

After lunch she headed out of Dunmore Street towards the Memorial Library to check their holdings. She had gone there first on the day she'd arrived, found it locked, read the hours, gone back then, found it locked again, and asked Maddy.

'They be open afternoons,' Maddy told her. 'Up to you to figure out which.'

So far Libby hadn't. But she went daily in the hope that one day she might. It was therefore with considerable satisfaction that she found the doors open when she got there that afternoon.

Feeling that the gods were smiling on her, she gathered the material she needed, sat down at one of the tables and began to read. She worked steadily through the afternoon, stopping only when it was time to meet Sam.

He came flying out of the school seconds after the bell rang, a grin splitting his gap-toothed face and Arthur close on his heels.

'Have a good day?' Libby asked.

'Uh-huh,' Sam said.

And Arthur asked, 'Can Sam come swimmin' with me down the dock?'

'Please?' Sam implored.

'Come home first and have a snack.'

Sam sighed. ''K. See you later,' he said to Arthur and fell into step beside his mother.

The day was hot and uncomfortably muggy. Rain during the night had only succeeded in making the humidity worse. Their house had fans but no air-conditioning, but the library had had neither so Libby was looking forward to getting home.

Until she opened the gate and saw Alec sitting on the doorstep.

# CHAPTER THREE

SLOWLY he got to his feet.

Sam, who hadn't noticed him yet, kept right on talking, telling Libby about their game of four square and what Sister had said when Arthur threw a spit wad at Mary Catherine. Libby didn't hear a word. She was watching Alec.

He was looking at Sam. And the expressions that crossed his face then were so many and varied that Libby couldn't even count them.

She wondered which one he would give voice to and prayed that, whichever it was, he would be discreet. She hadn't said that he shouldn't tell Sam, and she hoped to goodness now that he wouldn't blurt out anything that would hurt her son.

'Hello, Alec,' she said as coolly as she could manage.

He smiled. It was a faint smile, just the slightest lift of one corner of his mouth, and it made him look exactly the way Sam sometimes did in moments of stress and uncertainty. She swallowed hard.

'Hi,' Alec said.

Sam stopped talking, noting for the first time the man standing on the porch. He looked at his mother, expecting a response. Then, when she didn't speak, he smiled up at Alec. ''Lo. I'm Sam. Who're you?'

A look of pain flickered in Alec's eyes. He cleared his throat and looked at Libby. 'Aren't you going to introduce us?'

She drew a shaky breath. 'This is my son Sam.' She emphasised the 'my'. 'Sam, this is Alec Blanchard.'

'Hi,' Sam said again.

'Hi, Sam.' Alec said the boy's name softly as if he were tasting it, savouring it. 'Nice name. I like it. Suits you. Are you named after your father?'

Startled, Libby glared at him, but Sam just shook his head.

'My grandpa,' Sam replied.

'I named him after the man who stood by me when he was born,' Libby said bluntly, and felt considerable satisfaction at the spasm of anguish she saw on Alec's face. She unlocked the door and opened it.

'You go to school here?' Alec asked Sam curiously, noticing the book bag.

'Not usually. I live in Iowa. But it's sorta boring here when everybody else does, so I did, too.'

'You ought to come out and play with my little girl.'

Libby opened her mouth to protest, but Sam said first, 'A girl?' He looked doubtful.

Alec grinned. 'She's OK.'

Sam shrugged. 'Maybe.'

Libby almost said there was no way Sam was going to play with Alec's daughter, then thought better of it. If she objected, Sam would want to know why. It wasn't an explanation she wanted to make. Seeing father and son together made her vitally aware of a lifetime of complications she wasn't sure how to approach. She set her notebook and tape-recorder on the table and went into the kitchen. Sam and Alec followed.

'What do you want, Alec?' she asked him.

He met her gaze. 'You know that.'

She felt suddenly cold even in the mid-afternoon heat. 'I...'

'We'll discuss it,' he said, almost too pleasantly. Then, as if dismissing her, he turned to Sam.

'So, what do you usually do in the summer?' Alec asked him.

Sam shrugged. 'Play ball. Me 'n' Jeff and Greg go fishin' a lot.'

Alec looked at him closely. 'Jeff and Greg?'

'My uncles.'

Alec's eyes went to Libby. They were hard and questioning. 'Uncles?' His tone was sceptical, mocking.

'My brothers,' she said acidly.

'I see.' But she didn't think he believed her. Did he think she slept with a different man every night just because she'd been fool enough to sleep with him? She ground her teeth.

'And I go with my grandpa,' Sam went on, oblivious to the undercurrents in the room.

'What about your dad?' Alec persisted.

'Alec!' Libby said sharply.

Sam shrugged. 'I don't see him.'

'He doesn't need to,' Libby said, irritated beyond measure now. She whacked a slice off the coconut bread and handed it to Sam with a glass of milk. 'He's got plenty of men around just in my family.'

Sam looked from his mother to the man who was standing there staring at them both as if he'd suddenly caught wind of trouble. He hesitated a moment, then said stoutly, 'Mom's right. I don't need nobody else. I'm fine.'

Libby gave Alec a smug, satisfied look.

He didn't move an inch, not even to acknowledge that he'd heard.

The boy went on. 'An' here I go fishing with Arthur and his dad. We caught a shark day before yesterday,' he added. 'it was huge!' He threw his arms wide.

'That big?' Alec's voice was ragged.

'Bigger. Lyman says you can catch hu-mon-gous fish 'round here. We're goin' tomorrow.' He paused and considered the grim-faced man in front of him. 'You wanta come?'

'Alec is a very busy man, Sam,' Libby said quickly.

'I think I could manage it,' Alec said.

She gave him a hard stare.

He ignored her. 'If Lyman has room, of course.'

'What about your daughter?' Libby reminded him.

'She might like to come. It'd be good for her. She...' he paused as if looking for the right way to say something '...she needs to lighten up a bit.'

Sam looked mystified. 'Lighten up?'

'She's had a hard time this past year,' Alec said. 'Her mother died.'

'Oh.' Sam looked up from his milk and darted a quick worried look at his own mother. 'I'll bet she's sad.'

'Yeah, well, she hadn't seen her mother in a while.'

Libby looked at him closely, curiously, wondering if Alec was over Margo's death now. Probably not. If Clive Gilbert's had crushed him, how much worse would be the death of the woman he loved.

She found herself wondering what sort of life Alec and Margo and their daughter had led.

Had Margo followed Alec around while they left the child with nannies? It was possible, she supposed. Margo had never looked the maternal sort. She felt a pang of compassion for the little girl.

'What's her name?' Sam was asking.

'Juliet.'

'There's a Julie in my class in school. She's a pig. How old is yours?'

Alec grinned. 'Almost eight. And she's not a pig.'

'Well, I guess you can bring her, then,' Sam said. 'I'm seven and a half,' he added, wiping the back of his mouth with his hand.

'I know.'

Sam looked at him curiously. 'How d'you know?'

'Your mother said.'

Sam looked at Libby as if wondering what else she might have said to this stranger.

'I really wish you would come see her some time,' Alec told him. 'She needs kids to play with.'

Libby had had enough. She didn't know what Alec was trying to pull, but she was protecting her son no matter what. 'Here comes Arthur,' she said to Sam. 'You'd better get changed if you're going swimming with him.'

'Yeah, right. See you,' Sam said to Alec, and, grabbing another piece of coconut bread, he disappeared into his room.

'What,' Libby asked Alec in the silence that followed, 'are you trying to do?'

He had been staring after Sam, but now he turned to her. 'Get to know my son,' he said.

'*My* son,' Libby corrected.

'Mine, too. You told me so.'

'A biological accident. They happen.'

'Indeed they do,' Alec said with an edge to his voice. 'Indeed they do.'

Libby turned her back on him, staring out of the window, hating him, hating the way he made her feel.

He had no right to come here, no right to burst into her life again this way. And, especially, he had no right to Sam.

'When are you going to tell him? That I'm his father, I mean?'

Libby shrugged. 'Maybe I won't.'

'The hell you won't!'

Libby turned and stared at him. 'Why should I?'

'Because he has a right to know.'

She pressed her lips together in a tight line. That was true, of course. But it wasn't something you could spring on a child. It took handling, preparation. 'Some day,' she conceded finally. 'It isn't urgent.'

'I think it is.'

'*Now.* You didn't even know he existed until yesterday.'

Alec's jaw tightened. 'I know now. And I want to know him.'

'Bully for you.'

'Damn it, Libby. He's my son.'

'For how long? As long as it suits you? And then what?'

'It will always suit me.'

Libby shook her head. 'How do I know that?'

'You think I'd walk out on him?'

'You walked out on me.'

For a moment he just stared at her, a muscle working in his jaw, a fire flickering in his eyes. Then he raked savage fingers through his hair. 'I'm back.'

'Oh? That gives you rights?' She gave him a scornful look.

'Yes,' he bit out, 'it damned well does. I had a child with you and I have the right to be his father.'

'As far as I'm concerned you have no rights, Alec. You made your choice eight years ago.'

'Damn it, Libby, I couldn't——'

'You could. You did. Go away, Alec. Just go away.'

She prayed he would, that she would hear footsteps heading for the door, that it would shut behind him, that he would leave her now the way he'd left her all those years ago.

She heard silence. And then he came up softly behind her. She could feel the warmth of his body just inches from her. She stiffened. His hand touched her arm, and she jerked away. 'I said go.'

'Libby——'

'No, Alec. Leave me alone. You didn't want me. You don't want me. Just go!' She spun around now and glared at him.

'I do want you,' he said roughly. 'I always wanted you.'

Libby said a rude word.

'And you wanted me.'

'Well, I don't want you now!'

'Oh?' His voice was silky and slightly mocking. He ran his hand down her arm. She pushed him away.

'Damn you, Alec! Don't touch me.'

'I want to touch you.'

'And whatever Alec wants, Alec gets? Is that it?'

His mouth twisted bitterly. 'Don't I wish!'

'Been denied a lot, have you?' She didn't wait for an answer. 'Well, good,' she went on. 'Then this won't come as such a shock to you.'

'Be reasonable, Lib.'

'I am reasonable, Alec. You be reasonable now. You haven't been a part of my life for eight years. You were a brief fling, nothing more. You've never been a part of Sam's life. Why should I want you around now? What good would it do?'

'He'd know his father!'

Libby shook her head. 'I'm not sure that's good.'

'Libby!'

She shook her head stubbornly. 'I'm not.'

'Cripes, Libby. You can't expect me to just walk away, to take a look at my own flesh and blood and leave.'

'Yes, I can. I do.'

'I won't do it.'

'What are you going to do, then, Alec? Are you going to try to take him from me?' She flung it at him as a challenge, but the moment that she did there was a heart-stopping pause. She looked at him, horrified. 'You *can't* take him from me.' She sounded desperate and she knew it.

How could she help it? Damn Alec Blanchard, anyway. With all his power and fame, he probably thought he could have anything he wanted! Even her son.

Alec sighed again and shoved his fingers through his hair. 'I don't know what I can do yet. But I'm going to do something.' He shifted from one foot to the other, sounding infinitely weary.

She clenched her fists. 'I'll fight you every step of the way, Alec!'

He looked startled at her vehemence. 'Libby, for goodness' sake, calm down.'

'Calm down? You talk about taking my child away from me and you tell me to calm down!'

'I didn't talk about it. You did.'

'You didn't say you wouldn't.'

He shut his eyes. 'And I won't. Don't ask me to. I'm not walking out of his life. Not now. Not ever.'

'Alec . . .'

He shook his head adamantly. 'No. We'll sort it out.' He moved towards the door as if he was going to leave.

'I'm not going to let you walk on me, Alec. You're not going to just get whatever you want! I'll——'

He turned abruptly, facing her. 'We'll talk later, when you're rational.'

'I'm perfectly rational!'

'You're not.' He put his hand on the doorknob.

She came after him. 'Alec!'

'Not now, Lib. You wanted me to go, I'll go. For now.'

'For always,' she insisted. 'We don't need you. We don't want you.'

He let go of the doorknob and reached for her, taking hold of her arms with both his hands, turning her so that she was forced to look up into his eyes.

'But I want *you*, Libby. I mean that. Both of you. And I'll be back.'

\*   \*   \*

It was the stuff of which once dreams—and now night-mares—were made.

Eight years ago if Alec Blanchard had told her he wanted her and had looked at her with that proprietorial gaze, Libby would have been over the moon.

No longer. She'd had a whole night to think about those words, to mull them over, examine them, dissect them. And she knew what she felt now: distrust. And fear.

She knew it wasn't her he wanted, no matter how possessive his look, no matter how determined his words.

It was Sam.

And he meant it. She'd seen it in his eyes, in the way he watched the boy, the pained smile, the tender curiosity. The hunger. Mostly the hunger.

But what did he mean about wanting them both? He couldn't really want her? Except perhaps as a bed partner. They'd certainly been compatible in that way, Libby remembered, her cheeks burning. But he hadn't loved her. His leaving her for Margo, his marriage and his subsequent, 'I'll certainly forget about you,' were not the words of a man who'd ever really cared.

No, if he wanted her now it was only because she had been fun for a roll in the hay and because it was through her that he'd gain access to Sam.

She wanted to run. All her instincts told her to forget her commitment to Professor Dietrich, to forget every-thing except grabbing Sam and running as fast and as far as she could.

But common sense defeated instinct. She knew Alec. He would follow her to the ends of the earth if he wanted something from her.

Running would never keep her safe from Alec. If she wanted to keep Sam, she would have to stand her ground.

Alec Blanchard had a short attention span, she thought bitterly. She knew that from experience.

He couldn't stay on Harbour Island forever; he was one of the most sought-after directors in the business. Surely he was only here for a brief respite and would be gone in a matter of days. She could hold out against anything he might try for that long.

And if he lasted the summer, she and Sam could leave first. In Iowa she would be in a better position. She'd have the moral support of her family and friends.

But that didn't solve her immediate problem. Right now she needed to figure out how to handle Sam's invitation to Alec to join the fishing expedition this afternoon. What would happen if Alec actually showed up?

Would he—heaven forbid—tell Sam that he was his father?

Suddenly she had to talk to him again. She practically flew down the street and around the corner to Maddy's house.

'What's Alec's number, do you know?' she panted when Maddy opened the door.

Maddy's eyes widened, but she didn't ask any questions, just rattled it off.

'Thanks.' Libby was out of the door again almost at once.

'You want to use my phone?' Maddy called after her. But Libby just shook her head. She'd use a public one. She didn't need this conversation taking place—even just her half of it—in the middle of Maddy's kitchen.

Maddy's cousin, Lois, answered and Libby asked for Alec.

'Who's calling, please?'

Libby swallowed then, gave her name. If Lois was surprised, she gave no indication of it, and moments later Alec came to the phone. His surprise was obvious.

'Libby?'

'I . . . I just wanted to say, Alec—if you . . . if you go with Lyman fishing this afternoon . . . if you talk to Sam, you . . . can't tell him.'

He didn't pretend to misunderstand her. 'Then you tell him.'

'Not . . . not now. He wouldn't understand.'

'He's never going to understand any better.'

'I can't, Alec. Not now!'

'When?'

'I . . . I don't know.'

'Soon.'

'I'll . . . see.'

'You have to tell him some time, Libby.'

She didn't answer and her silence spoke for her.

He sighed. 'Be sensible, Libby.'

'I'm trying to be. I didn't want this, didn't want you here!'

'What we want and what we get are two different things.' Alec said bitterly.

'How would you know?'

'Believe me, Libby. I know.' There was a long pause. Then he said, 'All right. I won't tell him. Yet.'

'Thank you.'

'But I expect you to.'

'Mmm.'

'What are you afraid of, Lib?'

*You*, she wanted to scream. I'm afraid of you. You turned my life upside down eight years ago. I'm afraid of it happening again. I'm afraid of it happening to Sam, too. But she didn't say any of it. She said dully, 'I'll tell him when it's time, Alec.'

'Just do it,' he said. 'Or I will.'

She had to trust him, whether she wanted to or not. And she had to let Sam go, too. She could scarcely hide him away; Alec knew right where to find him. And, even if she'd wanted to, she couldn't think of a good reason to give Sam for keeping him home.

She certainly didn't want him to think there was more between her and Alec than there seemed. She knew that if she made a fuss she would have to tell him who Alec was.

And she wasn't ready for that. Some time she would. Some time when she felt safe, secure. When she was home again, married. With Michael.

Then she would tell him about Alec. But not now. Not yet. She didn't even know *how* to tell him.

It would have been different if Alec had known about him from the first. Then Sam would have grown up with an awareness of his father. He would have grown up understanding how his parents came to live apart.

But seven and a half years had passed during which he'd known nothing. For seven and a half years she'd raised Sam by herself because Alec hadn't wanted to know. He had no right now to burst into their lives.

Sam was her son, not Alec's. It was her right, not his, to decide when to let Sam know who his father was.

Besides, he was a little boy. He knew nothing about the pain grown-ups could inflict on one another. There would be time enough for that.

She saw him off with Arthur, waving and smiling, hiding all her trepidation, till he was far down the hill. Then she drew a deep breath, bit her lip and went off to interview one of the ladies who baked for the hotels.

Clara was in her late seventies, sharp as a tack, and had plenty of stories to tell. They sat on her porch and while Clara reminisced, Libby listened, fascinated, grateful for anything absorbing enough to take her mind off Alec and Sam. She would have kept listening until Lyman came back with the boys, but Clara yawned suddenly.

'That be plenty for now,' the old woman said with a smile. 'Don' want to wear you out.'

'May I come back?'

Clara patted her knee. 'Any time.'

She had just left Clara's when she heard footsteps behind her and a voice, an American voice, said, 'Excuse me.'

She turned to see a young man not much older than herself bearing down on her. He was smiling and he hurried to catch up when she paused.

'Wayne Maxwell,' he said, offering his hand.

'Libby Portman.'

He grinned. 'Thought you were a fellow American. What mag?'

'Mag?'

'Magazine. Aren't you a reporter, too?'

Libby shook her head.

Wayne looked at her doubtfully. 'I don't recognise you, but then I don't know everybody, I guess.' He sounded apologetic and somewhat surprised.

Libby shook her head, amused. 'I'm not a reporter. Really.'

'But you were tape-recording that old lady. Saw you yesterday, too, down by the dock talking to some fishermen.'

'I'm doing a research project.'

He laughed. 'Aren't we all? Blanchard's a hell of a project, isn't he?'

Libby swallowed. 'Blanchard?'

'Don't give me that,' Wayne chided her. 'You can 'fess up to me. We can help each other out.'

Libby shook her head. 'I'm a graduate student from Iowa. I'm doing an oral history project for my master's thesis.' She held out her notebook. 'Look.'

He took it and flipped through it, then looked up and shrugged, a rueful smile on his face. He handed the notebook back to her.

'Well, I'll be damned. You really aren't here dogging the famous director's footsteps.'

'No.' Not on your life.

Wayne grinned. 'Good. Means I can look at you as more than competition. Let me buy you a cup of coffee.'

There wasn't really any place to buy coffee, and Libby didn't want to be considered more than competition. But he seemed a nice enough man and, as long as he didn't know she had anything at all to do with Alec, there was no harm in chatting with him.

So she went along with him while he bought each of them a can of Pinder's Bahamian soda at the grocery. Then together they walked down to the dock.

Since he'd decided she wasn't competition, Wayne was quite open with her. 'Been here since last Sunday,' he said. 'Tried to get an interview right off with Blanchard. He won't see me, of course.'

'Why not?'

Wayne shrugged and settled down on the rough unpainted boards. 'Doesn't like the Press, our Mr Blanchard. "Too nosey," he says. "Life's private. Concentrate on my films," he says.'

Libby sat down beside him, staring out over the water to keep an eye out for Lyman's boat. 'Isn't that typical?'

'Probably,' Wayne said. 'It could be because of his wife's death.'

Libby frowned. 'What do you mean?'

'There was a reporter with her—driving her—when they crashed. Jerry Corson, his name was. They were heading down to LA to meet Blanchard. I guess Corson had talked Margo into a series of exclusives.' Wayne shook his head. 'Blanchard probably blames him.'

It was possible, Libby thought. She remembered Alec's reaction to Clive Gilbert's death, how much he'd blamed himself.

'He hasn't talked to the Press since.' Wayne sighed. 'It's been a year almost. Be nice to have a story.'

He would have one in spades, Libby thought, if he ever saw Sam and Alec together. And, as at this very moment she could see Lyman's boat approaching, she finished her soda and stood up. 'Thanks for the drink. It's been nice meeting you.'

Wayne got to his feet, too. 'You're welcome. Where are you off to now?'

'I have another interview up by the gaol. Want to walk along?' She hoped he would and was relieved when he fell into step beside her.

Libby didn't look back, even as she heard the boat coming nearer. She didn't know if Alec was even on board. She'd find out soon enough. She prayed that if he had been, he had kept his mouth shut. She wouldn't have to wait long, she was sure, to find that out, too.


'Your friend came with us,' Sam reported cheerfully when he came into the house, sunburnt and smiling, at suppertime.

Libby stopped ladling up the conch chowder. 'My friend?' she echoed. Not, *your father*?

'Alec,' Sam said. 'The guy who was here yesterday. And Juliet, too.'

Libby nodded, relief singing through her veins. He hadn't told. 'Alec's daughter?'

'Uh-huh.' Sam hoisted himself up on a stool and nibbled on a piece of the freshly baked bread Maddy always brought.

A bit of soup slopped on to the table as Libby set the bowl down. 'Is she . . . nice?'

Sam shrugged. 'She's OK. Didn't say nothin'. Just hung on him, y'know.'

Like her mother, Libby thought. The two times she'd seen Margo around Alec before the wedding, she'd attached herself like a barnacle to his arm. But she remembered that Alec certainly hadn't objected.

'Really?' she said vaguely, then changed the subject. 'Did you catch anything?'

Sam beamed. 'Tons. Lyman helped me clean 'em. We can freeze 'em, he says.'

After supper they did just that, with Sam chattering on about his day at school and fishing with Arthur, and Libby all the while mentally voicing a thousand questions about what Alec had done and what he'd said and what Sam thought of him.

She didn't say a word. If Sam volunteered, that was all right. She wasn't going to ask.

'Juliet isn't much of a sissy. She baited the hook when Lyman showed her,' he said, his tone respectful. 'But Alec had to help her pull her line in.'

Once he had done the same for her. They'd used hand-lines, the way Lyman always did. But while Alec had hauled in grouper and sergeant-fish and fish of every description that afternoon, Libby had sat there, her line slack, and wondered what he knew about fishing that she didn't. She hadn't really cared, though. Just being with him, watching him, talking to him, listening to him, had been good enough.

Then, all of a sudden, there'd been a sharp tug on her line.

'I've got one,' she'd said unnecessarily.

'Pull it in.' Alec was preoccupied with his own fish.

Libby pulled. The line cut into her hands. She wrapped it round and round, pulling harder, biting her lip. 'I think it's a whale,' she muttered.

Alec finished landing a small grouper and turned to laugh at her. 'Sure, Lib.'

She was panting now. Her arms hurt. The line was cutting off the circulation to her fingers.

'You want some help?'

She resisted at first, not wanting him to think she was a sissy. She fought the fish, struggled. The boat tipped crazily. And when it did that, Alec began to look concerned.

'It might be pretty big after all,' he conceded.

'Right,' Libby said through clenched teeth.

'You want to play him out a little?'

'What do you mean?'

'Loosen your hold. Let him run. Tire him. Then haul him back in.'

'Loosen the line?' She stared at him as if he'd uttered a blasphemy. 'Give up what little headway I've made?'

He grinned. 'Sometimes you have to. Only way to land 'em in the end.'

Libby wasn't convinced. But in the end, she gave him the line. He eased it out, let the fish fight away, then hauled him back, determined, patient, steady; inch by inch; bit by bit; hand over hand, Alec hauled it alongside the boat.

And when it surfaced they were staring down at a seven-foot nurse shark.

'Shall I?' Alec nodded towards the knife in the bottom of the boat.

Libby nodded and handed it to him. He cut the line and let it go.

'All that work for nothing,' she said, watching it disappear into the depths.

But Alec had shaken his head and rubbed his aching hands. 'Not really. It's the challenge.' He had turned to her with his eyes sparkling. 'I love a challenge.'

Was that what Alec was gearing up for now? Did he see getting involved with her and Sam as a challenge?

Was he, heaven forbid, relishing the thought of trying to haul them in?

What happened the next afternoon certainly created that impression. Libby was typing up her notes, keeping one ear open for the sound of Sam coming through the door after school. Instead she heard knocking and found Maddy on the porch holding out an ivory-coloured envelope. The spiky scrawl of her name and Sam's on the envelope was clearly Alec's.

She'd only seen his writing once, but once was enough. She felt a shiver of trepidation run down her spine.

Sam, pounding up from school just then, looked at her with wide-eyed interest. 'Who's it from? Mike?'

'No.' She read it silently. It was brief. Would she and Sam like to join him and his daughter for dinner the following evening?'

'Who?' Sam persisted.

'It's from Alec Blanchard,' she said flatly.

Sam looked puzzled. 'What's he writin' us for? He can just come down and talk to us, can't he?'

'He could,' Libby said. But she knew he wouldn't. It would be more subtle this way. And harder to refuse.

'What's he want?' Sam asked.

'He . . . invited us to dinner.'

'Great! I can see Juliet's garden.'

'It's my decision, Sam,' Libby said sharply.

Sam's eyes widened at her tone. Libby sighed guiltily. She didn't usually speak to him that way, not about dinner invitations at least. But invitations like this one were not as innocent as they looked.

She was afraid of what it implied, what Alec might do if they didn't accept, but even more of what might happen if they did. She wasn't immune to Alec, even now. He still had the power to make her heart beat faster, to make her pulses race.

And she was sure he knew it.

Alec used everything—and everyone—to his advantage. Libby didn't want it to be her.

'She has a tree-house,' Sam said. 'It'd be nice to climb in a tree-house.' Then, as if he knew when he'd pushed far enough, he added, 'I'm gonna play two square with Arthur,' and disappeared through the gate.

'What you going to do?' Maddy asked her when it shut after him.

Libby closed her eyes, shaking her head.

'You don't go, you show him you're scared.'

'I am scared.'

'He know that?'

'No!' She hoped not, at least.

Maddy shrugged ample shoulders. 'Why tell him, then?'

Libby sighed. 'I suppose you're right.'

'What's he doin'?'

'By inviting me, you mean?'

'Yup.'

'He says he wants me.' Libby said the words tonelessly.

Maddy considered them. 'You want him?'

'No!'

The older woman looked at her for a long moment, as if unable to decide whether to challenge that statement or not. Finally she decided to let it go. 'Best not want him,' Maddy said at last.

'I know.' It would be so easy—too easy—to fall back into the mindless love for Alec Blanchard that once she'd revelled in. But it would be a disaster if she did. She needed to be strong, resilient, and keep remembering Michael.

Maddy spread her hands. 'Then you got to show him. You got to be tough. For yourself and for the boy.'

'I know.' Libby sighed. 'And that means going, doesn't it?'

'Yup, it do.'

'So I will.'

# CHAPTER FOUR

'I THOUGHT we wouldn't go,' Sam confided as they walked up the road towards Alec's family's house. He had been surprised when Libby had told him her decision. He'd also looked pleased.

Libby wondered how to let him enjoy it and still not encourage a friendship between him and Alec. So far she hadn't had any good ideas.

'It's polite,' she said, striving for a non-commital tone.

'You don't like him, do you? Alec, I mean.'

Libby stopped in the centre of the tarmac and stared at her son. 'I like Alec fine.'

'Doesn't seem like it. You don't smile at him like you do at Michael. You don't even look at him.'

'He isn't Michael, Sam.'

Sam kicked the stone in his path and watched it skip along the road. 'You known him a long time?'

'Yes.'

'He likes you.'

Libby stumbled. 'Of course he likes me,' she said irritably.

'Same as Michael likes you, I mean.'

She stopped and stared. 'How do you know that?'

Sam looked guileless. 'I know. He asked lots of questions.'

'What sort of questions?' Libby demanded.

Sam shrugged. 'Where we live, what you do, are we happy, do you like what you're doing? Like he cares. 'Specially about "are you happy". What if he wants to marry you, too?'

'There is no way I'm marrying Alec Blanchard, Sam. I'm marrying Michael.'

Sam's eyes seemed to widen briefly at the vehemence of her answer. But then he shrugged again, apparently willing to accept her answer on faith. 'I like Michael, too,' he approved and kicked another stone, heading on along the road.

Libby watched him, worried more than ever now. Her nerves were stretched taut as piano wire the closer they got to Alec's sprawling glass and cypress house that sat high on the hill overlooking the trees and the turquoise ocean.

She could find a million reasons now that they shouldn't have come. Proving that she wasn't running scared seemed paltry in comparison.

But just then the road turned, and at the end she spotted the Blanchards' house peeking over the ornamental cement-block wall. Sitting on the wall there was a small blonde girl.

The moment the girl saw them, she waved at Sam, then turned to yell over her shoulder. 'Here they come! Daddy! Daddy, here they come!'

Unconsciously Libby slowed down. Sam, with no such hesitation, ran to meet her. Just before he reached the wall, the little girl hopped down, the gate opened and Alec appeared.

He was wearing a pair of blue and white canvas shorts and an open-necked short-sleeved white cotton shirt. His dark hair was still damp from the shower and his cheeks were smooth and ruddier than usual, as if he'd just shaved. He was tall and tanned and drop dead handsome. Worst of all, he was smiling right at her. The mere sight of him set Libby's heart to hammering.

She tried to steel herself, determined to remember the indifference she was determined to show.

Alec tousled Sam's hair and greeted him when the boy came in the gate, but his eyes never left Libby's. He held out his hand to her as she approached.

'You came.' His voice was soft, slightly rough. It sounded surprised almost.

She had been expecting him to gloat, was prepared for that. She wasn't prepared for hesitation on Alec's part, however brief. It took her a moment to recollect herself. She let him take her hand and deliberately pasted on a polite smile.

'It was nice of you to invite us,' she said in her best well-brought-up tone.

'Nice had nothing to do with it,' Alec drawled, and she knew that his momentary uncertainty had vanished. The gate shut behind her with an ominous click.

She glanced around wildly, ready to bolt. But Alec was still holding her hand, and she couldn't pull away. 'Relax, Lib,' he said mockingly, his thumb caressing her palm. 'I won't jump you right here.'

Then, as her face flamed, he drew her forward, saying, 'There's someone I'd like you to meet. This is Juliet. Juliet...' he turned to the little girl '...this is Sam's mother Libby.'

There was an oddly hopeful note in Alec's voice as he introduced them. 'Like each other,' he seemed to be saying.

Libby stared at him, amazed. Then, slowly, her gaze went to his daughter.

She'd felt pain at the thought of Alec's other child for eight years. She'd deliberately tried to put the child out of her mind. When she couldn't, she'd imagined a siren like Margo—an eight-year-old blonde temptress. The reality was far different.

Oh, she looked like her mother with her long blonde hair and her beautiful cheekbones and delicate chin. But she had none of the presence that Margo exuded. She was small, pale and, clearly, very shy.

If Juliet had seemed forthcoming enough with Sam, the moment Alec introduced her to Libby, she ducked behind her father and clung to his arm, looking at Libby warily. Libby felt a certain sympathy with her: it was the way she might have acted at that age. It was certainly the way she'd been tempted to act when she'd first met the stunning Margo.

Libby smiled at her and took a closer look, trying to find some of Alec in the child. She didn't see any.

Now she said quietly, 'Hello, Juliet.' Then, getting no response, she went on. 'Sam says you have a tree-house.'

The little girl nodded shyly.

'Did you build it?'

'I helped.' Her voice was as small and hesitant as she was.

'Can I see it, please? Now?' Sam broke in, bouncing from one foot to the other, a peasant to Juliet's princess.

Juliet looked at her father.

Alec nodded. 'Go ahead. But listen for Lois to ring the dinner-bell.'

Libby watched them go, her feelings mixed. She was glad that Sam had made a friend, was glad that the shy little girl seemed to like him as she seemed in need of a friend, too.

But the fact that she was Alec's daughter, Sam's half-sister... It didn't bear thinking about.

'Thank you,' Libby said when they were alone, 'for not telling him.'

Alec beckoned her in through the sliding glass doors that led from the deck into the living-room. 'I gather you haven't either.'

Libby followed slowly. 'No.'

'But you will.' He poured her a daiquiri and handed it to her. Libby didn't know if she was glad he remembered that she liked them or not. She took refuge behind the glass.

'Eventually.'

'We could do it together.'

'No.'

'I thought that's why you came tonight.'

She shook her head.

'Then why did you come?'

She shrugged awkwardly. 'Because I didn't want to explain to Sam,' she said finally. 'He'd want to know why I said no.'

'Somebody ought to explain to Sam.' Alec's voice had a hard edge to it now. He'd poured himself a whisky and his knuckles whitened around the glass he held. 'How much longer do you think he's going to be content to have a dad who's "away".'

'He's perfectly content.'

'His dad's not.' Alec walked back through the glass doors and stood staring out towards the sea.

'I don't care about his dad,' Libby said tightly.

Alec turned to stare at her, his dark eyes hard and bitter. 'You should.'

'Why?'

'Because life will be a lot more pleasant for all of us if you do.'

Libby's fingers tightened on the glass. 'What's that supposed to mean?'

He paused for a moment, then said evenly, 'I want to know my son.'

Libby took a sip of her drink. 'Maybe Sam won't want to know you.'

'Sam will.'

The confidence in his voice made Libby hate him. She glared, her heart slamming into her ribs, her mind whirling, her anger back. 'You're so sure, so confident. Damn you, Alec. I shouldn't have come!'

'On the contrary,' Alec said, 'it's a damned good thing you did. I'd have come looking for you, otherwise.'

Libby lifted her chin. 'To do what?' It was a dare. A challenge. A gauntlet thrown down. And the moment she'd said it, she knew it was a mistake.

He set his glass down on the railing and moved towards her purposefully.

Libby stepped back, her calves coming up sharp against the back of a deck-chair. 'No.'

'No? I don't believe that, Libby. I don't believe it for a moment. And neither do you.' And Alec's lips came down on hers, warm and gentle, and in her heart Libby heard the echo of a memory so sweet, so pure, so perfect that she wanted to cry.

She trembled, her eyes shut, her fingers clenched into tight, resisting fists. No! she thought. No! And still the kiss went on, deepening, persuading. No! Please, no! she begged.

And then, at last, Alec lifted his head and looked as shaken as she. Then the look was gone so quickly that she was sure she'd imagined it. A corner of his mouth lifted and he drawled softly, 'No, Libby?' He shook his head. 'It felt very much like yes to me.'

Her fingers clenched, she wrapped her arms tightly against her chest, refusing to look at him. She knew she was shivering. She didn't care.

He took a step back so that he was no longer touching her except with his eyes. He smiled. 'Shall we eat with the kids or would you prefer to wait and eat alone?'

It was so far from what she had expected him to say that Libby was struck dumb.

Had it meant nothing to him, then? Apparently it had. Otherwise he couldn't have just stood there unmoved, unshaken. She fought for her sanity, for the calm determination she so desperately needed.

'With them,' Libby said tonelessly when at last she could trust her voice.

He didn't object, nor did he refer in any way to the kiss. But there was a sense of satisfaction about him while he refilled Libby's glass, a sort of unspoken 'I told you so'.

'I'll just tell Lois,' he said and disappeared into the kitchen.

While he was gone she tried to compose herself, but she felt shattered. How could a man wreak havoc with just one kiss? Deliberately she took deep, even breaths.

When he returned she was standing on the veranda looking out across the tops of the trees towards the turquoise and purple waters of the Atlantic. He came to join her at the railing. She stepped back warily, but he showed no indication of wanting to pursue the kiss.

'I saw you with Maxwell yesterday,' he said, his voice hard.

'Who?'

'The reporter.' He looked at her closely. 'Didn't he tell you?'

'He told me.'

'You batting your lashes at him now?'

Libby stared. 'Am I what?'

Alec's mouth twisted. 'Flirting with him?'

'I most certainly am not.'

He gave her a hard look, then shrugged. 'You went off with him.'

'He wanted to talk to you. I didn't think the circumstances were propitious.'

'They weren't. They never are.' He stared out across the railing towards the ocean. 'Stay away from him.'

Libby stared at him, open-mouthed. 'I'll see whoever I like, damn you.'

'Not a reporter,' Alec said harshly.

'He seemed a nice man. Why don't you just talk to him?'

'I don't like reporters.'

'Because of . . . Margo?'

His head whipped around and he glared at her. 'What about Margo?'

'J-just that W-Wayne said she'd died when she was driving down to LA with a reporter. Th-that they were meeting you.' Libby regretted saying a word. She could see the pain on his face. It answered her question about how much he'd recovered from his wife's death. He hadn't.

He didn't say anything, but his lips tightened into a thin line and some nameless emotion seemed to flicker in his eyes.

'Stay away from reporters, Libby,' he said again. 'They're leeches, out for whatever they can get.'

'He only wants a story.'

Alec gave her a doubting look.

'It seems more sensible to give him one, that's all. Then he'll let you alone.'

'Can you guarantee that?'

'No, of course not.'

'Nor can anyone else. Even your nearest and dearest,' Alec said roughly.

Libby looked at him, wondering who had betrayed him in the past. She might have asked but Alec changed the subject abruptly.

'So, what do you think of Juliet?'

'She's . . . a lovely child.'

'She is. Margo has good children.'

'So do you,' Libby said quietly, unable to help herself.

The look he gave her was grim. He raked his hand through his hair. 'There's consolation for you,' he said bitterly.

Libby looked at him sharply. She saw an uncharacteristic vulnerability in his expression. It was the way he'd looked when she'd met him, the day Clive Gilbert's death had still been too much to bear. Was he thinking about Margo's death again?

Probably. Now she supposed he would want to confide in her about that. Well, he wasn't going to. She couldn't go through it again.

She turned away abruptly. 'I don't want to hear about it, Alec. If you want to talk about it, I'm sure Wayne Maxwell would be happy to listen. I'm not. It has nothing to do with me.'

'For goodness' sake, Libby——'

'I don't want to talk about it! If you insist, I'll leave.'

She could have taken it, she supposed, if it had been anyone but Margo whom he wanted to talk about. But there was nothing she wanted to know about his marriage to Margo Hesse, nothing that wouldn't just rake up old pain.

Alec pondered his glass for a moment. 'Did Sam tell you we went fishing with him?'

'Yes.'

'He's quite a kid. You've done well with him.'

'Thank you.'

'Was it . . . tough alone?'

'I've had lots of help.'

'Your brothers, you mean? And your parents? I always knew you came from a close family. I-I shouldn't have jumped to conclusions earlier,' he admitted.

'No, you shouldn't have.'

'How did they . . . take it when you . . . when you found out? Were they . . . ?'

He stopped, as if verbalising the question was too difficult. There was a tenseness in his face, a line of hectic colour along his cheekbones. Did it bother him, knowing what they must have thought of him?

She doubted it. And even if it did, too bad. It was nothing compared to what she'd gone through, not just with her family but with the whole town.

'My family were shocked when they found out,' Libby said frankly, telling it exactly as it was. 'I let them down, and I knew it. But they didn't let me down. They were there for me through everything.'

'Unlike me.'

Libby didn't say anything to that.

He rubbed his hand against the back of his neck. 'How was it? Your...pregnancy, I mean?' He had trouble with that word, too. 'Did you...have a hard time?'

Libby shrugged. 'I was sick a lot at first. But I was going to school so I didn't have time to pamper myself. And the actual delivery wasn't bad.'

'You were lucky.'

The look she gave him was ironic. 'Was I?'

He had the grace to blush and look away.

'Dinner's ready,' Lois said from the doorway, and Alec's relief was obvious.

'Everything looks wonderful, Lois,' Libby said when Maddy's cousin had served them conch fritters with peas and rice, fresh pineapple, green beans and, for dessert, key lime pie.

The food alone would have guaranteed Sam's good opinion. But Juliet's tree-house had enchanted him.

'You gotta see it, Mom,' he said, digging into the rice. 'We should build one like it when we get home—in the oak tree. Pop'd let me. I know it.' His eyes shone.

'Maybe.'

'He would.' Sam was positive.

'You live with your grandparents?' Alec asked him.

''Bout three blocks away. I go there a lot. My grandpa builds things for me. He made an airplane that really flies out of balsa wood. And my grandma bakes the best cookies.'

Juliet pushed her peas and rice around. 'I wish I had grandparents,' she said to her plate. They were the first words she had spoken during the meal.

Libby looked first at Juliet, then at Alec, surprised. She supposed that Leopold Hesse, Margo's peripatetic director father, might not settle anywhere long enough to be a real grandparent. But Alec's own parents were charming, down-to-earth people, the sort who would have doted on a grandchild.

'My father died six years ago,' Alec said, answering her unspoken question. 'Heart attack. And my mother passed away last fall.'

He couldn't keep the bleakness out of his voice, and Libby thought that that must account for the look on his face. She remembered how much he'd cared for them, how much they'd cared for him.

'I'm sorry.'

He nodded. 'Thanks.' Then, as if he couldn't talk about it any more, he turned to Sam. 'So, you want to go fishing again soon?'

Before Libby could protest Sam agreed eagerly. 'It was more fun with you. Lyman's sorta bossy otherwise.'

'Lyman knows what he's talking about.'

'I know,' Sam admitted.

The conversation that followed was, to Libby, bittersweet.

There was an obvious affinity between father and son—a connection she had hoped she'd imagined, but now knew was true.

She saw Juliet watching them both, then sneaking glances at her. But every time Libby ventured a smile, the little girl looked quickly away. But it wasn't a disdainful snub of the sort Margo had been capable of. It was shyness, pure and simple. She was the sort of daughter she—Libby—might have had.

Once again the unfortunate 'if only' smote her, and this time it was harder to shove away.

Deliberately she asked Alec about his work. 'Maddy says you've just finished a film.'

'On the contrary, it just about finished me.' He sighed and pushed his plate away, stretching, making Libby all too aware of the muscles flexing beneath his shirt.

She swallowed. 'Hard work?'

'Incompatible personalities. Natural disasters. Strikes. Rattlesnake bites. You name it.'

'I'm sure you prevailed.' She gave him a small smile.

He cocked his head. 'You've a great deal of faith in me.'

'I know you,' she said bluntly. 'You get what you want.' She kept her voice even.

'And I never let anything stand in my way. Is that what you're saying?' Alec's eyes narrowed.

She shook her head, determined not to be baited. 'I was only saying what I remembered.'

Alec gave her a long, speculative look. Libby kept her eyes on her plate.

After dinner, at Alec's suggestion, Juliet showed Sam her Lego and they built a rocket with Sam pestering Alec every few minutes for praise and advice. Finally Alec joined them on the floor.

Libby, watching as the two dark heads and one blonde one bent over the project, squabbling and consulting, teasing, grinning, felt an ache growing somewhere deep inside her.

Suddenly she wanted the evening to be over as badly as she wanted it to last forever.

It was just past nine when she could take it no longer. She stood abruptly. 'We have to go.'

Alec looked up from where he lounged on the floor. 'It's early yet.'

Libby shook her head and looked pointedly at a yawning Juliet. 'Not for the children. And Sam has to go to school tomorrow.'

Alec got to his feet. 'He could come up here and play with Juliet. She gets lonely. She'd like a friend.'

'No.' That was the last thing she wanted. 'He's going to school. He has friends there. If Juliet is lonely, why don't you send her?'

Juliet seemed almost to shrink at the suggestion.

'No.' Alec's tone was adamant, as negative as Libby's had just been. 'I want her with me,' he added in a more conciliatory tone.

Libby shrugged. 'Suit yourself. Come on, Sam. Thank you for the dinner.' She opened the door.

Alec held it for her, then followed her out. 'I'll walk you back.'

'It's quite unnecessary. I have a flashlight.'

'I'll walk you back.' His tone brooked no argument. 'Juliet——'

'Can get ready for bed. Lois won't leave till I come back.'

There was no way to change his mind. To try would be to make Sam wonder what her objection was. To try would be to let Alec know she was more wary of his effect on her than he knew. Libby shrugged and turned back for a moment. 'Goodnight, Juliet.'

A pair of wide blue eyes met hers for an instant. 'Night.'

Libby was halfway down the path when a little voice followed her. 'When are you coming back?'

She turned back, surprised. 'I don't know. But when Lois goes shopping some time, you come and see me.'

Juliet beamed for just a moment, then waved and shut the door.

'Don't say it if you don't mean it.' Alec loomed behind Libby in the darkness. Sam, carrying the light, scuffed on ahead.

Libby stopped and glared at him. 'Why wouldn't I mean it?'

'You don't have time for me.'

'You are not your daughter. I wouldn't hold anyone's parentage against them,' Libby said bluntly. 'Besides, I'm not the one who leads people on.'

He sucked in his breath and Libby thought she heard a curse on it, but all he said was, 'It's just that she's lost a lot. I don't want her to get her hopes up.'

'I only said to drop by.'

'I know that.' But from his voice she knew he thought that Juliet was pinning hopes on it, looking for far more than that.

'No,' Libby said aloud.

Alec frowned. 'No, what?'

She shook her head. 'Nothing.'

She tucked her hands into the pockets of her skirt and started walking again, quickly now, trying to catch up with Sam. The road was rough, more pot-holes than tarmac. She stumbled, and Alec's hand shot out, catching her the way he had caught her once before, the night she'd met him.

She yanked her hand away now. 'I'm fine.' And she began to run, not stopping until she caught up with Sam.

He stopped to wait for them at their gate, saying to Alec, 'You comin' fishing tomorrow?'

'I might.' Alec didn't look at Libby. He reached out a hand and touched Sam's hair. 'Night, sport.'

Sam grinned. 'Night, Alec. Thanks.' He disappeared through the gate.

With a quickly mumbled, 'Thanks again for dinner,' Libby made to follow.

Alec snagged her hand and held her fast. 'Don't.'

'I have to. I don't have a Lois to foist Sam off on,' Libby said.

'I don't "foist" Juliet. I told you, I want her with me. I take her damned near everywhere I go.'

'Sorry,' she said, still trying to free herself from his grasp. 'But, if I don't go in, Sam will dawdle. Goodnight.'

'One thing,' Alec insisted, still holding her wrist.

'What?'

'This.' He pulled her against him, one arm sliding around her back to hold her tight, the other hand coming up to cup her head so that their lips met perfectly. Just the way they had earlier, just as if a meal and three hours of conversation hadn't interrupted them.

Just as if eight years—one marriage and two children—had not gone by.

His lips were warm and persuasive, his tongue seeking, wanting. Libby knew what he sought, what he wanted— her traitorous body wanted it, too. Her mind might abhor him, her emotions might hate him. But her body recalled him all too well. And it craved what it remembered.

No, she told herself. No! But her will was weak. Her hunger was strong. It was only by forcing herself to remember the devastation she had felt when he left her, the pain at his blithe, 'Forget me. I'll forget you,' that she resisted him.

He'd married Margo, she told herself. He'd made his choice. He couldn't come back to her now. She couldn't—wouldn't—let him.

She pushed him away, sucking in a deep, desperate breath. 'Goodnight, Alec,' she said in the firmest, most indifferent voice she could manage.

She shut the gate in his face.

Sam was in bed when she went up to his room. He had the blanket pulled up to his chin and he was staring over the top of it, his brown eyes owlish in the dim light.

'Are you glad we went?' he asked her.

Libby rubbed her lips with the back of her hand, then managed a smile as she straightened his blanket. 'I hadn't seen the Blanchards' house in a long time. It was nice to go.'

'D'you like Juliet?'

'Of course.' Libby bent to pick up Sam's discarded shorts and shirt and held them in her arms.

'She's OK,' Sam allowed. 'For a girl. That tree-house really is great, though.'

Trust Sam to keep things in the proper perspective! She bent to kiss him.

Sam kissed her in return, throwing his arms around her, giving her a bone-crushing hug. Then, as she turned and walked towards the door, his voice followed her.

'I thought you were marrying Michael.'

Libby stopped dead, looking back over her shoulder. 'What?'

Sam grinned broadly. 'That was some kiss.'

Libby felt her face burn as she realised that, from his bedroom window, Sam had a perfect view over the top of the gate.

She glared. 'You know better than to spy on people.'

He sat up. 'I wasn't spyin'. I just looked out and...there you were. D'you s'pose he learned it from being in the movies?'

'Very likely,' Libby said, her voice dry. 'Go to sleep now, Sam.'

'What about Michael?'

'That kiss had nothing to do with me and Michael. The kiss was...for old times' sake, I guess.'

Sam looked doubtful, but then he shrugged. ''K.' He snuggled down under the blanket and said sleepily, 'I'll bet he lets me come see the tree-house again now.'

Chagrined, Libby went into her own room and stripped off her clothes, letting the breeze from the fan above cool her overheated body. She looked at herself in the mirror.

Her body was a woman's now. Fuller, softer than it had been when she had first known Alec. Eight years ago she had been coltish, all arms and legs, small hips and breasts. Her hips were wider now, her breasts, since nursing Sam, slightly rounder. She looked better, she thought.

She wondered what Alec thought.

Don't, she told herself. What Alec thought didn't matter. He probably would still find her attractive. The way he kissed her proved that. But it meant nothing. He didn't love her. He still loved his wife. His kisses were no more than lust and, perhaps, a misguided effort to get to Sam through her.

It was Sam he wanted, not her.

'What about Michael?' she asked herself aloud, echoing Sam's question. She made herself think about Michael, about going home and marrying him, about the life they'd share together. She tried to conjure up his craggy tanned face, his deep-set dark blue eyes.

But, perversely, the face she saw was brooding, dark, intense, not craggy. The eyes deep brown, not blue.

'Go away, Alec, damn you,' she muttered and, drawing the nightgown over her head, she put out the light and slipped between the sheets.

Congratulations, she told herself. You survived.

But later that night when a storm awakened her and the wind off the ocean seemed to whip through her soul, she said it again out loud. 'You survived.'

Though, she had to acknowledge, only just.

*       *       *

The next morning, as soon as she saw Sam off to school, she called Michael. 'Hi.'

'Libby?' He sounded astonished to hear her voice. She'd written every day, brief notes chronicling her research and general activities, but from the first she'd told him that phone calls were going to be scarce; it usually took too long to get through.

The wait didn't bother Libby this morning. She needed to talk to him. She had scarcely slept a wink all night. If she could just hear Michael's calm steady voice, feel his love echoing through the phone lines, she would be all right.

And it was a sign of God's approval of her actions, she decided, when she got a connection the first time.

'What's up?' Michael asked her, his tone worried.

She tried to sound breezy. 'N-nothing. I just...got lonely.'

'Glad to hear it.' He was cheerful, not apprehensive now. He sounded the way he always did, delighted to hear her voice. Calm, ordinary, sensible—the way she wanted to feel.

Talk to me, Michael, she thought. Soothe me. Make me forget the clamourings in my soul.

'You should go away more often,' he said, and she knew from his tone that he was smiling.

'Maybe.' But not if she ran into Alec.

'So tell me about it. Your letters don't do it justice, I'm sure. How's it going?'

'What? Oh, the research? It's all right.' She told him about her interviews. They always discussed their research with each other. His biological studies weren't so far removed from her oral history that they couldn't understand each other's work.

She wanted to tell him about Alec, but the longer they talked, the less she could find a way to say it.

Michael knew there'd been a man in her past—how couldn't he know, given Sam? But they'd never talked about the man whom Libby had loved. She'd always declined.

'It isn't important. It's finished,' she'd said over and over. 'Completely.'

And Michael had taken her at her word. 'You don't sound very certain,' he said now.

'What? Oh, my work you mean. I am. It is. It's fine. It's just that . . . well, I didn't realise how much I'd be missing you.'

She heard another sigh—of relief this time, she thought. 'Thank goodness,' he said. 'I miss you, too.'

She closed her eyes, imagining him sitting in his office, his feet up on the desk, the morning sun streaming through the window making prisms through the water of his aquariums.

'How's your work coming?' she asked him.

'I'm getting tons done with you gone. But it isn't worth it.'

'I wish you were here.'

'You do?'

'Of course.' Then, realising he really would start to worry about her if she continued to sound bereft, she added, 'But it won't be all that long until I'm home, I guess. I'm looking forward to it.'

'Me, too. How's Sam? Is he there now?'

'He's doing wonderfully. He's at school and I'm on my way to the dock to a straw shop for an interview. I'm calling from a public phone. There isn't one at the house.'

'So there really isn't any way to reach you?'

'No.'

'I'll find a way,' he said.

'Huh?'

'Never mind,' Michael replied. 'I'm just thinking out loud.'

Libby heard bells ringing in the background and realised the time. 'I promised to meet Martha at nine-thirty. I'd better run.'

'Right,' Michael agreed. 'See you.'

'Six weeks and six days,' Libby promised.

But Michael had already hung up.

# CHAPTER FIVE

IF LIBBY thought that invoking Michael's presence
through a phone call was going to solve her problem,
she was wrong. And in case she had trouble perceiving
it herself, Alec was only too happy to show her.

She finished interviewing Martha at her front-porch
straw market and was walking up Colebrook Street when
she met Alec coming down.

'Have lunch with me.' It was less an invitation than
a command.

Libby shook her head and kept walking. 'I'm busy.'

He fell into step alongside her. 'I can see,' he said,
his tone mocking.

'I am.' She waved her notebook and tape-recorder in
front of his face. 'I've been on an interview all morning.
I have to transcribe my notes.'

'How long will that take?'

'An hour. Maybe more.'

He glanced at his watch. 'OK. You transcribe. I'll fix
lunch.'

'I——'

'You have to eat, Libby. Everyone does. So stop being
an idiot and come on.'

He took her arm and, short of digging in her heels
and starting a fight with him right in the middle of the
town, in front of God and all the chickens, Libby could
only allow herself to be dragged.

He didn't make the mistake of trying to get her to his
house, and she could hardly resist being taken to hers.
But, if she'd entertained the notion of shutting the gate

in his face again this afternoon, one look at the grim set of his mouth and the determined thrust of his jaw told her she wasn't going to get away with that manoeuvre a second time.

'Where's Wayne Maxwell?' she asked him, hoping that the mere mention of the reporter would make him release her.

'Gone,' he said tersely.

'Chased him out, did you?'

'Would you want him to get a look at me with Sam?'

No, Libby didn't want that. She shook her head.

'So be glad he's gone.'

She guessed she was. But she hadn't thought that Wayne was a bad guy. If anyone was going to write a story about her, she'd want it to be someone like him. She said so.

And Alec replied, 'Yeah, well, I gave him a bit. That make you happy?'

'I guess.'

He gave her a hard look. 'Good,' he said and strode on, hauling her in his wake.

Once they were in the house, Alec pointed her towards the typewriter set up on the dining-table. 'Go to it,' he said and, giving her a gentle push, he turned and headed for the kitchen.

Irritated, Libby watched him go. 'Good luck,' she muttered under her breath.

Lunch for her was rarely more than a piece of fresh pineapple or some left-over fish from last night's dinner. Since Sam hadn't been there to demand his perennial peanut butter and jelly sandwich, she'd had no desire to fix anything at all and consequently kept little on hand.

She heard Alec rummaging through the refrigerator, banging cupboards, opening drawers.

'I don't hear you typing,' he called.

Libby jumped. Guiltily she flipped the cover off the typewriter and sat down. The last thing she wanted was for Alec to find her standing there right where he'd left her like some awestruck groupie.

She opened her notepad, rolled a sheet of paper into the typewriter, turned on the tape-recorder and began to type.

Concentrating, however, was a different story altogether.

The most scrumptious smells began to waft her way. The pop and sizzle of something cooking enticed her. Libby's stomach growled, her mouth watered. Sighing, she flipped off the tape-recorder and, despite her better judgement, her feet made their way towards the kitchen.

Alec was stirring something in a frying-pan. He looked up when she appeared in the doorway. A corner of his mouth quirked. 'That hungry, are you?'

'Mmm.'

He grinned. 'You didn't have much to work with.'

'I didn't think anyone was going to be poking through my groceries,' Libby retorted. 'Besides, I don't usually eat lunch.'

'You should.' His eyes skated over her from neck to toes. 'You're too skinny.'

'I'm thin.'

'Too damned thin. Your hips are fuller, but there's no meat on you. You were just right before.'

Libby, hating his appraisal, turned away. 'I was barely eighteen.'

Alec drew a long breath. 'I know. That was one of the problems.' He jabbed at the food in the frying-pan.

'It didn't seem to bother you at the time,' Libby said bitterly.

'The more fool I,' Alec rasped. 'But,' he added, 'you're not a child now, are you?'

'No, I'm not,' Libby said evenly.

'So the stakes have changed.'

She frowned. 'What stakes?'

'It isn't just fun and games this time, Libby.'

If she'd ever wanted verbal confirmation of how he'd felt about their lovemaking, now she had it. Her jaw tightened and her fists clenched. She willed herself not to react, not to show him she cared.

He took another swipe at the mixture in the pan. 'Set the table,' he said brusquely. 'Lunch is ready.'

Lunch was a stir-fry of left-over fish and shrimp, some green onion and green pepper, soy sauce and ginger, peas and rice. It was filling and remarkably tasty, or Libby was sure it would have been had she been able to appreciate it.

She was still smarting from his 'fun and games' remark, still trying to get herself under control.

She was wholly unprepared when Alec shoved back his plate and looked at her squarely. His fingers drummed for a moment on the table-top, then stilled. His dark eyes locked with hers. 'Marry me, Libby.'

It was the last thing she expected him to say.

She simply gaped.

'Marry you? You're joking!'

'No.'

'I wouldn't have you if you were the last man on earth!' she said, her eyes flashing.

'Why not?' He didn't sound surprised, just determined.

Libby laid down her fork and met his gaze. 'One,' she said with every bit as much determination in her voice as she'd heard in his, 'I don't want to; two, I don't love you; and three, I'm marrying someone else.'

One and two, she knew, wouldn't have made him even pause for thought. Three seemed momentarily to stun him.

'Marrying...? Who?' he demanded.

'You wouldn't know him.' She picked up her fork again.

'*Who, damn it?*'

She didn't imagine she was hearing jealousy in his tone, only annoyance that someone else might dare to claim what he thought was his own. She took a sip of coffee. 'He's a professor at the university.'

'What's his name?'

'What difference does it make?'

Alec slapped his hands on the table-top. 'I don't know, damn you. Just tell me his name!'

Libby just looked at him. 'Why? Are you going to go intimidate him?'

'Could I?'

Probably, Libby thought, if you glared at him like that. 'No,' she said.

'Then tell me. If he's going to be stepfather to my kid, I have a right to know.'

'You have no rights at all, Alec.'

He sucked in a sharp breath. 'Damn you.' His eyes glinted dangerously. 'You're lying, Libby. There isn't anyone, is there? You're just saying it to put me off.'

'I'm not "just saying" anything,' Libby said. She finished her stir-fry and drained her mug, smacking it down on the table as she stood up.

Alec got to his feet. 'Yes, you are. You're trying to hold me off. You're afraid of what you feel for me.'

'What I feel for you, Alec, is nothing more than disgust. I was a fool for getting involved with you in the first place. I'm glad you married Margo. It saved you from doing the honourable thing and marrying me!' She brushed past him and went into the living-room, jerking open the door. 'Now just go away, leave me alone and stay the hell out of my life!'

Alec stood in the doorway to the kitchen simply watching her, waiting, making her wait. And finally, when she had no choice but to turn around and face him, he shook his head.

'I'm not going anywhere, Lib. Besides, you don't hate me. You couldn't kiss me the way you do if you hated me.'

Libby said a very rude word.

Alec scowled. 'Don't talk like that! You never used to talk like that.'

'I never used to do a lot of things.' Libby lifted her chin defiantly. 'This is the new me.'

'Ah, but the old you is still there, too, Lib,' Alec said as he moved towards her.

Carefully, as casually as she dared, she backed away. 'No, she's not.'

He smiled. 'I'll find her.'

'You won't.'

He caught her chin in his hand and lifted it so that she was forced to look into his eyes. He grinned, proving that, whether she had changed or not, he was definitely the old Alec. 'Count on it, Lib. I'm sure as hell going to give it a try.'

Everywhere she went, there he was.

He materialised in the library whenever she was writing—though how he knew what the hours were when she had had to badger the librarian to get them, she didn't know; he lurked on the beach when she and Sam went for a swim. He and Juliet went fishing with Lyman, Sam and Arthur; they invited Sam back to their house to cook the fish afterwards.

Libby, of course, was invited as well.

She didn't want either of them to go and found excuse after excuse, until Alec showed up on the doorstep one evening with Sam and Juliet in tow, a line of fish in his hand.

'Come on,' he said without ceremony. 'You and Sam are having dinner with us.'

And when Libby demurred he simply shrugged. 'Fine, then, we're having dinner with you.'

Short of throwing a tantrum there was nothing she could do. Alec simply strode in and took over, filleting the fish himself with the help of Sam and Juliet, while Libby was deputised to peel potatoes.

He was a surprisingly good cook, which she did not admit aloud. He took it as given anyway. 'Does what's-his-name cook for you?' he asked her while he worked over the fish.

'Sometimes.' Michael wasn't an enthusiastic cook, but he had on occasion done a bit. He did, however, take Libby and Sam out for a pizza or to one of the local eateries now and then.

'What's his name?'

She still hadn't told him and the fact seemed to gall him.

'What's whose name?' Sam asked.

Libby didn't speak.

Alec said, 'The man your mother thinks she's going to marry.'

His tone made Libby grit her teeth. The glare she gave him could have nailed him to the wall.

'Michael, you mean?' Sam offered.

Alec looked at Libby. 'Michael, is it? Michael who?'

'Garner,' Sam supplied again.

'He's a professor?' Alec made it sound like a dirty word.

Sam nodded blithely. 'He teaches biology. That's about frogs an' stuff. Him and me raised frogs last year. I mean we got the eggs—spawn, it's called,' he told Alec with grave authority. 'And we put fresh pond water in almost every day, and pretty soon we had tadpoles and they got bigger an' bigger, and then they started to get legs an' their tails fell off an', you know what, we had frogs. It was neat.' He looked at Libby for confirmation.

She sighed and nodded. 'It was.'

The envy on Alec's face was obvious—not because Sam had raised tadpoles, but because Michael had been the one to do it with him.

'Could we do that some time, Daddy?' Juliet asked him.

Alec gave a jerky nod. 'We'll try, sugar.' With unnecessary force he slapped the fish into the pan in which he was broiling them. 'Aren't you done with those potatoes yet?'

'Almost,' Libby said with false sweetness. 'I haven't had all the help you've had.'

'It sounds to me,' Alec said darkly, 'as if you've had more than enough help.'

Periodically throughout the evening the conversation came back to Michael. Libby didn't offer any information. The less Alec knew, the less ammunition he'd have to fight with. But she hadn't told Sam that, and Sam was dismayingly forthcoming. He chattered on at length about Michael, about how Michael took him out into the woods and taught him the names of the trees and shrubs, about how Michael had helped him dissect a grasshopper, about how, whenever Michael went on a field trip, he brought Sam back specimens.

Libby watched Alec get grimmer and grimmer. She watched his jaw tighten, watched a nerve twitch in his cheek.

'Veritable paragon, isn't he?' he muttered so only Libby could hear as he and Juliet prepared to leave.

'He's a wonderful man.'

Alec opened his mouth, then clamped his teeth shut on whatever he'd been about to say. The look he gave Libby was icy cold.

'I'll see you tomorrow,' he said at last.

'Don't bother,' she replied. 'I've got lots of work to do. I don't need distractions.'

He smiled then. 'Ah, but I want to, Libby. I dearly want to distract you.'

Seven days passed during which he appeared at least two and sometimes as many as five times a day. He swam with her, talked to her, walked with her, ate with her. He joked with Sam, played catch with Sam, went fishing with Sam.

In short he did everything she'd once wished he would do.

But it was a fantasy world, not the real one. Libby didn't trust it—didn't trust *him*—and wouldn't have even if she hadn't been engaged to Michael.

There were few places to go to avoid him. Being trapped on a tiny island with a man determined to make his presence felt was not easy. Especially because he evoked in her so many of the sensations he had eight years before. She was still attracted to him physically. He could still make her heart beat faster, her pulse hum.

But she was determined to resist him, and resist him she would.

It was with considerable relish, then, that she discovered the need to go to Spanish Wells for the day. One particular old fisherman, Gibb Sawyer, had come up in her interviews over and over.

'You must talk to Gibb, he'll know,' said Martha at the straw shop when Libby asked about a particular shipbuilding period.

'Ask Gibb Sawyer,' said Ambrose, another of the fishermen.

'Go see Gibb,' Travis Walker at the grocery told her.

Gibb Sawyer was well into his eighties now. And, according to everyone on Harbour Island, he was the best man with a story.

'Ole Gibb'll tell you everything,' they said.

'Lived here most of his life,' Martha told her. 'Went to live with his daughter over in Spanish Wells jus' last year. You talk to him.'

And when at least eight other people had said the same thing to her, it was time, Libby thought, that she went.

She was delighted. A day away. Time away from the relentless attention of Alec Blanchard. Time to think, to reassess, re-gird, regroup. A whole day of not having to look over her shoulder.

She made arrangements to take Sam out of school for the day and asked Lyman to take them.

'In the morning,' she told him. 'And come back in the evening. I want to take Sam around to see a bit of Spanish Wells, too. Can you do it?'

Lyman nodded. 'Meet you at the dock at nine.'

But when Libby and Sam arrived at five past nine the following morning, it wasn't Lyman who was waiting.

It was Alec. And Juliet. The two of them sitting in Lyman's boat.

Libby stopped dead in the centre of the dock, teeth clenching, fists curling in the face of Alec's smile.

'Lyman got a job,' he said with perfect equanimity. 'Got a chance to crew on one of the big boats docked at Valentine's this morning. I said I'd fill in.'

Chance to crew, my foot, Libby thought. He'd been bought off. 'We can go another day.' She started to turn back.

'Sawyer's expecting you, isn't he?'

'I'll call him, arrange another meeting.' She said over her shoulder.

'He won't be there,' Alec said to her back.

Libby stopped and turned, giving him a narrow look. 'What?'

'Lyman heard he was going out on a fishing expedition tomorrow. Ten days or two weeks, he thought.'

Libby bristled. 'The man is eighty-six years old, Alec. I hardly think——'

Alec shook his head, smiling up at her. 'Amazing, isn't it?' He gave an equable shrug. 'Apparently he likes to keep his hand in. Going on his son-in-law's boat.'

'Tomorrow?'

'That's what I heard.'

'It's truly astonishing how much you hear, Alec,' Libby said with false sweetness.

Innocence personified, Alec smiled. 'A good director always keeps his ear to the ground.'

'I'm surprised you don't get your head stepped on more often,' Libby muttered through her teeth.

'What?'

'Nothing.'

He waited, watching her, and she knew he could see every angry emotion she felt. He probably even enjoyed them. Damn him.

And if she did walk away and set up another time, she knew what would happen. Lyman would get another 'chance' to crew on someone's boat. At the rate things were going, Lyman might crew all summer. Good for Lyman. Not so good for her.

And if, by chance, Lyman could be persuaded to take her, there wasn't a snowball's chance in hell that Gibb Sawyer would be available. Alec would see to that.

No. It was clear enough that Alec was directing this show. The circumstances were all going his way.

But Libby was damned if she was going to let him write her lines.

She met his gaze but not his smile. 'All right,' she said flatly. 'Let's go.'

It was impossible, however, to remain entirely stiff-necked and disapproving in the face of Sam and Juliet's whole-hearted enthusiasm as the boat left the harbour. They hung over the sides of Lyman's old outboard,

pointing out reefs and rocks, spotting turtles and schools
of fish as the boat skimmed northward, then turned west
to curve around the top of Eleuthera.

'Wow, look!' Sam shouted over the noise of the
engine.

Libby sucked in her breath. Sam was pointing at a
perfectly curved bay with a white sand beach and a line
of palm trees for a background. It presented a visual
Eden from afar.

It had certain idyllic qualities when visited too, Libby
remembered all too well. Quickly she turned away.

'Can't we stop? Please, can't we stop?' Juliet begged.

'Please?' echoed Sam.

Libby waited, holding her breath, expecting Alec to
make a sharp turn with the boat. He wasn't above that
sort of deliberate manipulation, heaven knew.

But he steered a steady course. 'Not now,' he said to
Sam. 'Your mother has work to do.'

Libby slanted him a glance and saw his sharp strained
features. He didn't look at her.

Was it possible, Libby wondered, that Alec was as un-
willing to face the memories as she was?

She glanced again towards the back of the boat, but
she couldn't read his expression. He was staring straight
ahead, his hand on the rudder, his face hard, his eyes
squinting into the sunlit sea.

'But it's so beautiful, Daddy,' Juliet wailed.

'First things first,' Alec said flatly. 'And first we're
going to Spanish Wells.'

Spanish Wells was just as Libby remembered it. A
small sun-baked hamlet, its fleet of fishing boats were
strung out along the quay and its pastel-coloured houses
rode a low hump of land in the middle of the island.
The school, post office and scattered shops were, she
knew, on the far side of the hump, overlooking a shallow,
crystal-clear bay.

'Do you know where to find Sawyer?' Alec asked as he anchored the boat.

'His daughter gave me directions.'

'You go on, then. I'll do some exploring with the kids.'

'Sam can——'

'Sam can come with me.'

She considered arguing, then shrugged. Sam would be happier roaming with Alec than sitting with her. She'd save her strength for the fights that mattered.

'When should we meet you?' Alec asked.

'I should be done by noon.'

'Fine.' Taking Sam and Juliet by the hand, Alec walked down the quay.

Libby looked after him for a long moment, struck by how right he looked with a child clinging to each hand, as if they belonged there.

She shut her eyes. It was folly to even think it, a curse to wish that it might have happened.

Gibb Sawyer, in a wheelchair, didn't look to Libby as if he was about to set out on two weeks' worth of fishing.

He said right off, 'So you want some reminiscing, do you? All I get any more. Ain't been out'na a boat since '84. Miss it, I do.'

Alec, you fiend! she thought to herself.

Sawyer raked a hand through thick white hair that had once been blond. His deep-set eyes sparkled an ocean blue. 'Sit a spell, then, 'n' I'll tell you what I know. Mag,' he said to his daughter. 'We could use somethin' cool t'drink.'

Over glasses of Mag's iced tea and a plate of ginger-snaps, Gibb Sawyer held forth. He talked about the boom years, the boat-building, the days when Harbour Island and Dunmore Town had prospered then waned. He talked about the fat years and the lean years, the storms and the sunny days. He regaled her with tales of a full and loving life, of a fifty-two-year marriage that

# *DOUBLE* YOUR
# ACTION PLAY...

# *"ROLL A DOUBLE!"*

Peel off label
place inside

# CLAIM UP TO 4 BOOKS
# PLUS A LOVELY
# "KEY TO YOUR HEART"
# PENDANT NECKLACE
# ABSOLUTELY FREE!

# *SEE INSIDE..*

# NO RISK, NO OBLIGATION TO BUY...NOW OR EVER!

## GUARANTEED

### PLAY "ROLL A DOUBLE" AND GET AS MANY AS FIVE GIFTS!

## HERE'S HOW TO PLAY:

1. Peel off label from front cover. Place it in space provided at right. With a coin, carefully scratch off the silver dice. This makes you eligible to receive two or more free books, and possibly another gift, depending on what is revealed beneath the scratch-off area.

2. You'll receive brand-new Harlequin Presents® novels. When you return this card, we'll rush you the books and gift you qualify for ABSOLUTELY FREE!

3. Then, if we don't hear from you, every month, we'll send you 6 additional novels to read and enjoy. You can return them and owe nothing, but if you decide to keep them, you'll pay only $2.49 per book—a saving of 40¢ each off the cover price.

4. When you subscribe to the Harlequin Reader Service®, you'll also get our newsletter, as well as additional free gifts from time to time.

5. You must be completely satisfied. You may cancel at any time simply by sending us a note or a shipping statement marked ''cancel'' or by returning any shipment to us at our expense.

The Austrian crystal sparkles like a diamond! And it's carefully set in a romantic "Key to Your Heart" pendant on a generous 18" chain. The entire necklace is yours free as added thanks for giving our Reader Service a try!

DETACH AND MAIL CARD TODAY!

# HARLEQUIN "NO RISK" GUARANTEE

- You're not required to buy a single book—ever!
- You must be completely satisfied or you may cancel at any time simply by sending us a note or shipping statement marked "cancel" or by returning any shipment to us at our cost. Either way, you will receive no more books; you'll have no obligation to buy.
- The free books and gift you claimed on this "Roll A Double" offer remain yours to keep no matter what you decide.

If offer card is missing, please write to: Harlequin Reader Service, 3010 Walden Ave., P.O. Box 1867, Buffalo, NY 14269-1867

DETACH AND MAIL CARD TODAY!

**BUSINESS REPLY MAIL**
FIRST CLASS MAIL   PERMIT NO. 717   BUFFALO, NY

POSTAGE WILL BE PAID BY ADDRESSEE

**HARLEQUIN READER SERVICE**
3010 WALDEN AVE
PO BOX 1867
BUFFALO NY 14240-9952

NO POSTAGE
NECESSARY
IF MAILED
IN THE
UNITED STATES

had only ended last year with the death of his wife. And when he spoke of her, Libby heard the love in his voice.

She wrote frantically, glad for her tape-recorder, grateful that he'd agreed to let her use it.

She lost all track of time, trapped by the sheer power of Sawyer's ability to tell a story, to make the people of Harbour Island of fifty, sixty, even seventy years ago come alive.

It was a shock to both of them, then, when, just as he was getting to the high point of a hurricane story, Mag appeared in the doorway of the tiny lounge in which they'd been sitting and cleared her throat. 'Visitors,' she said.

Libby looked around to see Alec and the kids standing behind her. She glanced for the first time at her watch. It was one-fifteen.

'Oh, heavens. I'm sorry.'

'No problem,' Alec said easily. 'Just wanted to tell you we're just going to get some lunch. We'll stop back.'

Gibb Sawyer shook his head. 'No, sir, you won't. 'Bout talked her out for one day, I have. You go on 'n' take her now. You'll be back, won't you?' he asked Libby.

She nodded. 'I wouldn't miss it for the world. But you can't leave me hanging here, either. I mean, you've got to finish telling me about the hurricane at least.' She shot an apologetic glance at Alec.

He shrugged equably. 'Go ahead. It's what we came for. We'll wait.' And before she could even introduce him, he herded the kids outside again.

'He's understanding, your man. Makes allowances. Only way to be,' Gibb said. He gave Libby a wink. 'You got a good 'un there.'

'He's not——'

'Make a good pair, the two of you,' Gibb went on over her protest. 'You fair, him dark. The boy like him, the girl like you. Yes, sir, a right good pair. Now, where was I?'

Libby stammered for a moment, stunned at his conclusion, about to correct him, then figuring it wasn't worth it. She said simply, 'The night the roof blew off the market.'

'Ah, right, I remember.' And, settling back against his wheelchair, Gibb finished the tale.

Libby arranged to come back and see him the following Monday. Then she thanked Mag for the tea and left. Alec and the children were waiting across the road watching a pair of goat kids frolic in a yard.

'Ready now?'

Libby nodded. 'I'm sorry I ran late.'

'We had a good time. We watched them weigh the catch and asked about the scuba facilities. Then we looked through the market and bought some biscuits. And when you still didn't show, we watched a bunch of ladies quilt.'

'You saw everything, in other words,' Libby said with a half-smile.

Alec grinned. 'Just about.'

'We bought groceries, too,' Sam told her, hopping from one foot to the other. ''Cause Juliet and me wanted a picnic.'

'I didn't see any place I was dying to eat lunch in,' Alec apologised. 'So when they begged...' He shrugged.

They were so eager, so enthusiastic. And a picnic did sound good. The day wasn't as hot as many had been. The breeze off the ocean kept things reasonable, and the humidity was relatively low. Besides, this Alec was easier on the nerves than the one who needled her constantly. This one was perhaps more insidious, but certainly much more comfortable to be around.

'Sounds great,' Libby said. 'Where?'

'The Swiss Family Robinson place,' Sam said at once.

'Yeah! Please?' That was Juliet.

Libby looked daggers at Alec.

He shrugged equably, his smile mocking her. 'What do you say?'

She wanted to say no. She wanted to say never. *I can't go back. Not there. I can't—won't—let myself remember.*

'C'mon, Mom, please?' Sam pleaded.

'It's so-o-o-o beautiful,' Juliet said. 'I'll remember it forever.'

Yes, Libby thought. *She* would, too.

She met Alec's gaze, shaking her head slowly, help-lessly, unable to answer. 'I want to go someplace else.'

But in the end, of course, there was no place else. Only there.

She had been eighteen and in love with the most won-derful man in the world.

What's more, he'd loved her.

So when Alec had asked Mrs Braden if that Wednesday, on Libby's day off, she could have the evening off as well, Libby felt as if she'd gone to heaven.

Mrs Braden wasn't sure. 'You don't want to make too much of this...business with Alec,' she cautioned Libby when they were alone. 'He's much older than you. As well as very—shall we say—experienced.'

'I know.' But in her head Libby thought, *he's only eight years older than I am. And if his more extensive experience doesn't matter to him, it certainly doesn't matter to me.*

'You'll be careful?' Mrs Braden asked, concern evident on her motherly face.

Libby smiled confidently. 'Of course.'

Mrs Braden reached out and brushed a lock of Libby's hair away from her cheek. 'I don't want him to hurt you, dear.'

'He won't,' Libby said with complete assurance. 'I like Alec. We're friends.'

Mrs Braden smiled ruefully. 'All right, then,' she agreed.

'I trust you to behave,' she said to Alec when he came to pick Libby up. Her eyes spoke volumes about responsibility and good sense as she saw the two of them to the door.

Alec grinned at her. 'You should,' he said. 'Trust me, I mean.'

'Should I?' Libby asked him as he led her down the path through the woods towards the road.

He turned her in his arms and kissed her hard. 'What do you think?'

Libby thought Alec Blanchard was the epitome of manhood, the hero of all her dreams, the man she would follow to the ends of the earth. She would have trusted him with her life.

He had, over the few weeks she had known him, become her best friend in all the world. After the night of their first meeting he had come seeking her out. He'd appeared on the beach again when she was there with Tony and Alicia. He'd swum with them, built sand-castles with them, added bits to the flotsam and jetsam sculpture on the beach with them.

And when Tony and Alicia were in bed and Mr and Mrs Braden were having drinks, playing bridge and talking with holiday-makers, Alec came to talk to her.

Together they walked on the beach or sat on the deck and he talked to her about his goals, his hopes, his dreams. Then he listened when she talked about hers.

Libby had never known a man so interested in her before. And she'd never met a man who so willingly trusted her with his deepest thoughts and emotions.

She was, she realised quite soon, the only one he ever talked to about Clive Gilbert. Clive's death had shaken him far more than he ever told anyone else. Only she had seen his face stark with pain, his eyes full of unshed tears.

'It's my fault. It should have been me,' he'd told Libby achingly one evening when they'd sat on the Bradens' deck in the darkness.

And Libby, putting her arms around him and holding him close, had thanked heaven that it hadn't been, even though she understood the guilt and anguish Alec felt.

'I owe him one and I can never repay him,' Alec went on, shaking his head. 'Never.'

Libby kissed him gently. 'Some day,' she'd said softly, her hands kneading his back, her lips caressing his cheek. 'Maybe some day you'll find a way.'

Besides sharing his feelings of guilt with her, he told her more. In fact, in the three weeks she had known him, she had learned more about him than she knew about the boys she'd grown up with, Danny whom she'd gone steady with, Cliff whom just two months ago she'd thought she wanted to marry.

But now she knew there was only one man in the world she wanted to marry—Alec.

She hoped—she dreamed—that he wanted to marry her.

They'd never had a real date, never been alone together for more than a couple of hours at a time. Until today.

'I borrowed Lyman's boat,' Alec told her as they walked out to the fishermen's dock. 'I want to take you somewhere special.'

'Where?'

He smiled and helped her into the boat. 'You'll see.'

Alec steered them across the reefs towards the north shore of Eleuthera, past Mar Island and around the tip of Current Point, staying close to the shore. Then they headed south again as they came around Bridge Point and Libby caught her first glimpse of the most beautiful little deserted bay she'd ever seen.

It was sheltered on three sides by a grove of palms, its broad beach a sandy pink and white powder, its waters a clear and warm mix of turquoise and azure blue.

She simply stared, a smile lighting her face.

'I thought you'd like it,' Alec said softly as the boat slipped into the bay and he cut back the engine.

'It's a Garden of Eden,' Libby whispered. 'I didn't think such places really existed.'

But that day proved they did.

Alec had brought a picnic lunch—lobster salad, hard rolls, fresh pineapple, a bottle of wine. And they had shared it, sitting beneath the palms, looking at the sky and the sand and the sea and, mostly, into each other's eyes.

They swam, frolicking in the water with the abandon of a couple of children. Libby, normally constrained by her nanny role, rediscovered the unfettered joys of play for the first time that summer.

Grinning mischievously, Alec splashed her, and she ran after him, shrieking and laughing, tackling him when the waist-high water slowed him down. But the feel of his hard sleek body beneath her hands drove all thoughts of horseplay from Libby's mind.

Alec turned in her arms, staggering to his feet, his own arms around her, his mouth hungry on hers, seeking and finding. Libby clung to him, desperate with longing, wanting him, needing him, unable to say a word.

Then he swung her up into his arms and carried her through the water and across the sand to where the blanket lay.

He put her down gently and knelt over her, his head shielding her eyes from the sun. His gaze was intent, his face taut with desire as his hands stroked first her hair and then her shoulders. Libby felt a tremor in them, felt one in herself wherever they touched.

'I'm supposed to behave,' Alec said thickly, his hands still moving, caressing, stroking. He was touching her arms now, her ribcage, the concave curve of her belly.

'Aren't you? Behaving, I mean.' Libby's voice was so tremulous she scarcely recognised it.

He gave a shaky laugh. 'I guess it depends on your definition.'

She smiled and reached up, letting her fingers trail down his hair-roughened chest. 'In my dictionary you're behaving beautifully.'

'Oh, Lib.' His voice was strangled, and then he bent to capture her lips again. 'Oh lord, I need you.'

And Libby needed him. She needed him more than she'd ever needed anyone or anything on earth. He made her alive, he made her complete; he was the other half of her soul.

Alec's hands slid the straps of her thin cotton top off her shoulders. His thumbs teased the line of her collarbone, then moved lower as his fingers eased the wet fabric away from her breasts.

Libby lay absolutely still, her eyes never leaving him, watching the expressions as they flickered across his face. She saw need, she saw hunger, she saw vulnerability. This last was never so clear as when he lifted his gaze to meet hers.

His eyes asked, they beseeched; they didn't demand.

And Libby lifted her torso away from the blanket, reached back and unhooked the clasp and let her top fall away.

Alec sucked in his breath. 'Beautiful. So beautiful.'

Libby smiled. 'You're beautiful, too,' she whispered.

A corner of his mouth lifted. 'Yeah, right.'

'You are,' she insisted. 'The most beautiful man I've ever seen.'

'You've seen lots, have you?' Alec's voice had a ragged edge to it.

Libby flushed. 'Not . . . everything,' she admitted.

One brow lifted. 'No?'

She shook her head, not meeting his eyes.

His hand came out to lift her chin. He was smiling. 'Good.'

'I want to,' she said fiercely and touched him again. Her hands ran down possessively over his chest and curled, her fingers sliding inside the waistband of his swimming-trunks.

It was bold, far bolder than she'd ever been—could ever have imagined herself being. But Alec brought out a side of her she'd never experienced before. He made her feel like a woman. She wanted to know him in his fullness as a man.

'Lib?' The one syllable echoed hoarsely.

Libby nodded and came to her knees so that her breasts brushed against his chest. She swallowed hard and so did he.

His forehead came down to rest against hers. Above the sound of the slap of waves against the shore she could almost hear the thunder of his heart in his chest.

He touched his lips to hers, and when they opened to the pressure of his mouth, he was lost.

'I want you, Libby,' he muttered.

And then his hands skimmed the bottom of her bathing-suit down her legs, and his own suit swiftly followed.

She wanted to see, but only felt. She wanted to touch and was touched instead. Alec's hands roamed over her body, teased her and tempted her, made her writhe with longing for him. And when at last she could take no more and reached for him, he covered her.

'It'll hurt, Lib,' he whispered.

She shook her head. 'No.'

And it didn't. Not then. Then she thought only of Alec, of loving him, of showing him that love.

She welcomed him fiercely, glorying in the strength of his thrusts within her, meeting him with a furious hunger of her own. She'd never felt like this before, had never experienced such need, such desire.

It built like waves build, surging, growing, lifting. And just when she thought there could be no more, an awareness burst within her, a shuddering climax enveloped her, and with Alec shuddering on top of her, the feeling broke as a wave breaks on the shore.

The feeling ebbed that way too. Slowly, like the tide, with soft swirls of longing, gentle lapping, tender touches. And Libby sighed, sated, pleased, justified.

She touched Alec's cheek. He lifted his head away from her shoulder and looked deeply into her eyes. He touched his lips to the palm of her hand.

'Are you all right?' he asked her.

'I am wonderful,' Libby told him. 'And so are you.'

He smiled, his features almost boyish. 'Because you make me that way.'

'I think,' Libby told him, 'it's mutual.'

They loved again in the waning afternoon sun. They swam lazily. They hugged. They kissed. And only when the sun began to set in the west did Alec load the boat and boost Libby in.

'It's our place,' Libby said. 'Our idyll.'

'Our Eden,' Alec agreed with her, starting the motor.

'Will we come back?' Libby asked as she watched the bay recede, the palm trees silhouetted against the orange and purple sky.

'You'd better believe it.'

And Libby, with Alec's arm around her to ward off the cool evening breeze, with Alec's love to warm her on the homeward trek, believed they would.

They never had.

# CHAPTER SIX

UNTIL now.

In eight years nothing had changed; and everything had. It was the same beach, the same sand, the same water, the same sun. The same man. It was a different world.

It was no longer Eden, no matter what Juliet said. But you couldn't have told either child that.

'It's like a fairy-tale place,' Juliet announced when Alec cut the motor and dropped the anchor over the side.

'Swiss Family Robinson could have lived here,' Sam said.

Libby expected Alec to agree, but when she looked at him he was concentrating on securing the anchor. Libby busied herself with the grocery bag, with the blanket, with making sure she had plenty of sunscreen to put on the children and a visor for herself.

'Last one on shore's a rotten egg,' Sam yelled and dived over the side.

Juliet, shrieking, followed him.

Libby started after her, but Alec reached for the grocery bag. 'Let me help you.'

Libby resisted, clinging to it. 'I don't want your help. I can manage.' She set the bag down, preparing to get it again when she'd got in the water.

'Suit yourself,' Alec said easily.

'Thank you,' Libby said stiffly in reply. She slipped over the side into the water and found it deeper than she'd thought. It lapped her breasts, and when she turned

106

to get the sack out of the boat, it was out of reach. She looked helplessly at Alec. There was a moment's silence while their eyes met, hers apprehensive, his mocking. Then at last he handed it to her.

'Thank you.'

'My pleasure.' He followed, bringing the blanket, carrying it down the beach and spreading it out on the sand.

Libby carried over the groceries, set them down and proceeded to lay things out carefully and deliberately.

She was continually aware of his eyes watching every move she made. Finally, when all conceivable avenues of distraction had been explored, when all means of ignoring him had been exhausted, she turned her back, staring out at the water, concentrating on Juliet and Sam.

They were dashing in and out of the water, laughing, hollering, Sam with his usual boisterousness, Juliet with more animation than Libby had ever seen in her.

She recalled Gibb Sawyer's words. She saw the children as he had seen them—a boy for Alec, a girl for her—and felt a shaft of pain so strong it almost knocked her off her feet.

She would have loved to have had a daughter like Juliet. For eight years she had resisted all knowledge of this child of Alec's and Margo's, had hated her the way she'd hated Juliet's father. She'd never imagined feeling this way about a child of their love. But now she couldn't imagine a world without Juliet in it.

She dared a peek at Alec out of the corner of her eye. Surely, even wanting Sam the way he did, he couldn't regret his marriage to Margo and the daughter who'd been born of it. She wondered what he was thinking.

'I wonder what Sam would say if he knew he was conceived under that tree over there,' he said.

Libby choked, then stared.

Alec met her gaze defiantly. 'He was.'

'I know that. But I don't intend to announce it. And you'd better not either.'

'I think I've already gleaned your feelings about that. Wrong-headed as they may be.'

'They're not! They——'

'They perpetuate a lie.'

'They make life liveable,' Libby argued.

'Matter of opinion. I wonder, Lib, do you lie to yourself as well?'

She glared at him. 'What's that supposed to mean?'

'Just what I said. Are you going to try to pretend you've never been here before? Going to try to forget the way it was?' The look he gave her probed her soul. 'You can't forget,' Alec said. 'Can you?'

She shrugged, determinedly indifferent.

'Can you?' he persisted.

'I don't *want* to remember,' she said harshly.

'Don't you?' The quality of his voice changed. There was still mockery in it, to be sure. But there was more. There was a sort of ache now, as if her reluctance hurt him.

'Did you?' Libby countered.

'For years I came back in my mind almost daily.'

Libby blinked, then opened her mouth, but no sound came out. She simply stared at him. Did he mean what she thought he meant?

A corner of his mouth lifted. 'I don't suppose you believe that,' he said heavily. 'But it's true.'

She wouldn't let herself believe it. She *couldn't* let herself believe it. To do so would be to undermine the very soul of her resistance to him.

He turned and let his gaze rest on Sam and Juliet. 'It isn't the way I'd ever dreamed of it, that's for sure— you and me here with a couple of rug rats.' His smile changed from rueful to almost happy. 'But I like it. It feels right.'

The quiet certainty in his tone was unnerving. And Libby looked at him anew, seeing how very much Alec had changed.

He wasn't a young man any more. At thirty-four he was in the prime of his life. He was strong, tough, powerful, determined—all the things she'd seen incipient in him eight years before. But he was also warm, steady, paternal.

Once she had loved the Alec he had been. She was afraid that if he continued this way she might learn to love this Alec, too. And that would be disastrous. Because Alec didn't really love her. He only wanted the son he thought she'd kept from him.

She wrapped her arms tight against herself, defending herself against him, against herself.

'Come on,' he said now, reaching for her hand. 'The kids shouldn't have all the fun.'

'I don't want——' Libby began, but Alec would have none of it.

'Damn it, Libby, lighten up. You want the kids to think there's something wrong?'

'There is something wrong,' she insisted.

He shook his head. 'Feels right to me.' And he grabbed her hand without giving her a chance to deny him. 'Come on.'

It would be a memory, Libby decided. A fairy-tale. One of those afternoons out of time which really don't have an effect on the reality of one's life. One day when the 'might have been's and 'if only's came alive instead of existing as mere dreams.

One day, she told herself. One simple day. A person couldn't ruin her life in one day as long as she knew that, like a fairy-tale, it would be over at midnight, if not sooner.

Her problem eight years ago had been confusing fantasy with reality. She wouldn't do that now. She knew who she was, where she was going, and with whom. She had Alec Blanchard in perspective now. She could handle him.

'All right,' she said slowly, and let herself go.

The afternoon was magical. The children came clamouring out of the water, wanting her and Alec to swim with them. But Juliet's hair kept falling in her eyes until Libby sat cross-legged on the sand and braided it so that it wouldn't snarl.

Together, like mother and daughter, they sat and watched Alec take Sam on to his back and swim out into the bay. He ducked under so that only his nose and the top of his sleek dark head were visible and blew bubbles as he approached the shore, making Juliet giggle and laugh.

Later the four of them built a sand-castle, then wrote their names in the sand and watched the waves erase them. They ate the sandwiches that Alec had bought in Spanish Wells, supplementing them with warm, fizzy cans of drink and sticky melting chocolate biscuits. Afterwards they licked the chocolate from their fingers, then ran into the water again. Libby felt happy for the first time in ages. It was amazing, she thought, what a little bit of fantasy could do.

By the time the sun had dipped into the west and the breeze off the ocean picked up, she didn't demur when Alec put his arm across her shoulders as they walked back into the water.

And after he helped her into the boat and draped a towel over his shoulder, he kept her close. The warm, wonderful feeling stayed close, too. And Libby found herself wanting to cling to it, preserve it, like the peaches she and her mother canned, to take out and savour when winter came once again.

It was the same insidious joy that had pervaded her soul the last time they had left Ben Bay.

But when they'd docked that time, there, waiting for them, had been Margo.

But there would be no Margo tonight. The fairy-tale would play itself out with the proper ending this time.

When at last the boat cruised slowly up towards the dock and Alec reached to tie it to its mooring, a flashlight beam gleamed in the darkness.

'Ah, Lyman?' Alec said. 'Catch.'

'Got it,' said a voice, but it wasn't Lyman.

It was Michael.

'Surprised you, didn't I?' Michael was beaming as he lounged back in the rattan sofa looking up at Libby, a cold beer in his hand.

'Stunned me,' Libby admitted, still stunned for that matter, and it had been two hours since she'd heard his voice coming out of the darkness. She was standing in the doorway to the kitchen now, carrying a glass of iced tea for herself, looking down at Michael with some of the same astonishment she'd felt at that moment.

She wasn't the only one who'd been amazed.

Sam had yelped, 'Is that you, Mike?' and had practically leaped from the boat into Michael's waiting arms. 'It is you!' The boy was clearly delighted.

And it was from his perch in Michael's arms that Sam had done the introductions. Libby couldn't have done them to save her life.

'This is my friend Juliet,' Sam said cheerfully. 'And Alec.' Then as Libby angled the flashlight up into their faces, Sam hugged the bearded man holding him aloft. 'This,' he told them, 'is Michael.'

Her arcing flashlight caught a kaleidoscope of impressions. She saw Michael, first grinning then looking curious as his gaze went to Alec whose arm was still around Libby. She saw Sam, overjoyed, Juliet open-mouthed, and Alec——

Alec was white as a sheet.

'Tie it off,' he said tersely to Michael and bent to grab the blankets and toss them on to the dock. He practically shoved Libby up, then handed Juliet out to her.

'Up you go,' he said briskly to his daughter as he clambered out after her. He manoeuvred her away from Libby, stepping between them. 'Did you plan it this way?' he demanded.

'I——'

'Because it doesn't matter if you did,' he went on harshly. 'It isn't going to make a damned bit of difference.'

'What——?'

'So you might as well send him home in the morning.'

If Michael's arrival hadn't already done it, the sheer audacity of Alec's remarks would have brought Libby down to earth with a thud.

'How dare you?'

'Oh, I dare, sweetheart,' he said so only she could hear. 'I dare a hell of a lot. Come on,' he said to Juliet, 'it's getting late. Time for bed.'

He gathered up all his gear, tossed a terse, 'See you,' over his shoulder and steered Juliet up the dock towards the road.

Libby stared after him until the darkness swallowed him up. His 'See you' rang in her ears, sounding far more like a threat than a promise.

'Night, Alec,' Sam called after him.

'Alec?' Michael dropped quietly into the silence. It was a question, but what it asked Libby wasn't sure.

'He...he's...his daughter is Sam's friend.' It was the best she could do. She began to rustle her belongings together, too. 'Take this, will you?' She handed a beach towel to Michael.

He took it. 'I see,' he said.

But Libby had no idea how much he'd seen until she'd tucked a sleepy, happy Sam up into bed and had come back downstairs.

Michael took her into his arms then and kissed her. It was a hungry kiss, warm and persuasive. And Libby wanted to be persuaded. She wanted to give herself to him with the whole-heartedness he deserved. But much as she tried, all she could remember was the way Alec had kissed her, the possessive passion which always flared between them and with which hers and Michael's couldn't compare.

Damn, she thought. Oh, damn! And the realisation made her want to cry.

Michael stepped back and looked at her, his expression worried, wary. 'Lib?'

But Libby looked away, unable to meet his eyes. 'I'm... tired. Sorry, I...' Her voice drifted off vaguely. 'Can I get you a beer?'

Michael shrugged, willing to wait. 'Sounds good.'

So she got him one, and a glass of iced tea for herself, and now they were facing each other once again.

'Shouldn't I have come, then?' Michael asked her, his grin fading, his voice soft.

'Huh? No. I mean, yes. I—I'm delighted you came. Just surprised, that's all.'

'Right.' His tone was dry. He took a long swallow of the beer, then stared at the glass, swirling the amber liquid as if he wasn't sure how to proceed. Then apparently he decided there was no way round the issue, only through.

He looked up and met Libby's eyes. 'Alec isn't only Juliet's father, is he?'

She felt the blood drain from her face. 'What?'

'He's Sam's father, too, isn't he?'

As long as the words were never spoken she could have continued to pretend. But there was no longer time for pretence, no longer room for the lies Alec had accused her of trying to tell herself just this afternoon.

Of course Michael had seen it. Anyone could. 'That doesn't change anything!'

'No?' Michael gave a snort of disbelief. 'Damn it, Libby! Why didn't you tell me?'

She paced the room. 'I couldn't. Anyway,' she sighed wearily, 'you're not the fool. I am.'

Michael shook his head. 'Why? Is he why you came here?' he asked her. 'Did you want to see if he'd have you back?'

'No! Of course not! I'm engaged to you! I didn't even know he was going to be here! I certainly didn't want him here!'

'It was just a coincidence, huh?'

'Yes.' She sat down in the chair opposite him, her fingers clenching round the glass.

'But he is Sam's father.'

Libby closed her eyes. 'Yes.'

Michael sighed. 'What's his name, Sam's father?' He seemed to need to keep saying it, hammering it home. 'Alec what?'

Libby swallowed, licked her lips. 'Blanchard.'

Michael goggled at her. '*Alec Blanchard? The* Alec Blanchard? That was Alec Blanchard?'

Libby nodded miserably.

'Lord.' He was looking at her as if he'd never seen her before. His brows were drawn together, his mouth pinched. He raked his fingers through his hair. 'Where'd you know Alec Blanchard from?'

'Here,' Libby said simply. 'I came here years ago. As a nanny. Before I went to college.' She'd never talked about it before to anyone other than her parents.

'So that's how you knew about the island. I wondered. How long were you here?'

'Just the summer. I worked for a family named Braden.'

'And Blanchard? Where does he fit in?'

'His parents lived here, too. He came to visit them. It was right after his first directing job.'

'*Glory Field?*'

'Yes.'

Michael leaned forward, forearms resting on his knees, his hands loosely clasped. 'I remember it. Smashing movie. Did everything, didn't he? Directed, acted. Even co-wrote the screenplay.'

'Yes.'

'There was a scandal, though...' Michael's forehead furrowed. Then he shook his head, unable to bring up the exact event. 'Somebody got killed?' he ventured.

She nodded. 'A stunt man.'

His face cleared. 'Right. I remember now. Terrible.'

'It was,' Libby agreed quietly.

Something in her voice made him look at her closely. 'Did you know the guy?'

She shook her head. 'No, he'd been killed right before I met Alec. But it was...it was very hard on him.'

Michael didn't say anything then, just looked at her. In the darkness she heard a frog croaking and the putt-putt of a moke as it chugged down the street.

'You knew him well.' The moment he said it, Michael gave a short, harsh laugh. 'What am I saying? Obviously you knew him well. Better than well.'

'I...'

'You loved him.' He flung the words at her, daring her to contradict them.

She couldn't. She met his eyes for a brief moment, then ducked her head. 'Yes.' It was a whisper, nothing more.

Michael sighed, slumping back against the sofa. 'And you've loved him for—what?—eight years?'

'No.' She lifted her eyes again and met his gaze fiercely now. 'I didn't. I haven't. I don't. I didn't want anything more to do with him. I didn't expect to see him here when I came. I expected to put it to rest.'

'Tell me.' Michael leaned back, his eyes on her, challenging, waiting.

She knotted her fingers. 'I was a child then, you see. Just eighteen. It was an infatuation. So when I came back I thought that then I'd be able to put it behind me and come home to you.'

'Dare I hope, then,' Michael asked drily, 'that today was just a little hair of the dog that bit you?'

Libby looked at him, bewildered.

'Cure for a hangover,' Michael explained. 'Another taste of the stuff that did you in the night before.'

It was a crude notion, but Libby had to admit that there might be some truth in it. 'Does it work?' she asked hopefully.

Michael grimaced. 'Supposed to.' He crossed an ankle over to rest it on the other knee. 'Doesn't look as if it has for you.'

'I haven't... I didn't...' Libby protested, but then her voice trailed off.

'Glad to hear it,' Michael said wryly.

Libby couldn't look at him. She heard him take another sip of beer, then set the bottle down again and get to his feet. She heard his footsteps on the tile floor. She saw the toes of his shoes as he came to stand in front of her.

'Lib?' He reached down and pulled her, unresisting, to her feet.

'Oh, Mike, I'm sorry! I didn't mean for you to walk into this!'

'I walked into it of my own accord,' he reminded her.

'Yes, but it shouldn't have happened. It——'

'Shh. It's not important. As long as it's over.'

'It's over,' Libby vowed.

He smiled. 'Then relax.' He put his arms around her and drew her close, hugging her.

And Libby let herself be hugged. She relished the secure warm feel of Michael's arms around her and the hard strength of his chest against her head. It was the way she always felt with him—safe, secure, beloved.

There was none of the passion she felt with Alec. There was none of the pain.

'Oh, Mike, what am I going to do?'

'Go to bed.'

She looked up at him confused. 'About Alec, I mean.'

He shrugged. 'Ignore him.'

Ignore him. Was it possible? Libby wondered.

'We'll talk about it in the morning. Nothing's going to change before then.'

'I suppose,' Libby said doubtfully.

He dropped a kiss on her forehead and stepped back. 'I'm sure of it. Unless, of course, I can tempt you into letting me into your bed?'

Libby shook her head.

Michael grinned ruefully. 'I was afraid of that.' He sighed. 'Don't worry, Lib. Just because he's wealthy and powerful, it doesn't mean he can run your life.' And he moved around her, heading up the stairs to the bedroom she had told him he could share with Sam.

Didn't it? Miserably Libby watched him go. All the joy, all the happiness, all the euphoria she'd felt that evening had vanished as if it had been no more sub-stantial than a puff of smoke.

It was what you got, she told herself savagely, for even for one minute allowing yourself to believe in fairy-tales. Why had she been such a fool?

*   *   *

She spent a sleepless night and came downstairs the next morning to find Michael already sitting at the breakfast-table, nursing a cup of coffee.

He gave her an encouraging smile. 'Morning.'

Libby nodded wordlessly and poured one for herself. Her head pounded. Her eyes felt gritty. Her mind was as shredded as a pad of steel wool.

'Still fretting?' Michael asked her.

'Mmm.'

He got up and put his arms around her. 'Don't. Entertain me. Show me the island. Blanchard won't bother you.'

Michael didn't know Alec.

He was on the doorstep almost before they'd finished breakfast.

'I came to meet your friend,' he said blithely to Libby when she gaped at him. And he brushed past her into the living-room before she could protest.

'Sam tells me you and he raised frogs together last year,' Alec said to Michael, finding him in the kitchen.

'That's right.'

Alec pulled out a chair and dropped into it. 'Thanks.'

One of Michael's eyebrows lifted. Libby made a strangled sound.

Alec shrugged. 'I'm sure he needed a bit of fatherly companionship then.' His voice trailed off; his meaning didn't. It was perfectly clear: Sam doesn't need it now. I'm here.

'I'll show you the island,' he offered. 'Libby has work to do.'

'I don't——' Libby began.

'She doesn't have much time,' Alec cut in. 'She needs every moment. She's always telling me so.' He gave her a conspiratorial smile that made her want to deck him. 'I've got a moke outside. Come on.'

Michael looked from Libby to Alec and back again, then shrugged. 'Sounds fine.'

After Alec had taken Michael on a tour of the island, he and Juliet took him to the beach to go snorkelling. Then they picked up Sam at school and dropped by Libby's long enough to tell her that they had reservations for dinner at one of the inns.

'Get dressed up,' Alec said imperiously.

'I was planning dinner for us here,' Libby argued.

'Not tonight,' Alec said implacably.

Sighing, Libby went. Alec entertained them royally, playing hot-shot director, impressing the usually unimpressionable Michael with his anecdotes and charm, plying him with brandy and good food and, not coincidentally, Libby was sure, keeping him clear on the other side of the table from her.

He didn't even let them sit together in the moke. He stuck Michael in the back with the kids while he and Libby sat up front. It was past ten at night when he finally dropped them off at Libby's house. And Libby was sure if he could have thought of a way to come in with them, he would have.

Michael thought it was all somewhat amusing. He kept looking at Libby now and shaking his head.

'What did he say to you?' she demanded.

'Warned me off,' Michael said, still grinning as he flopped down on the sofa.

Libby sputtered. 'Warned you off? Off me?'

'That's the general idea. He wants you back.'

Libby said a rude word. 'He just wants Sam.'

'I'm not sure about that.'

'I am,' Libby said darkly.

Michael's grin vanished. He reached for her and pulled her down into his lap, holding her so he could look her squarely in the eyes. 'The question isn't whether he wants

you or not, Lib. He does. The question is, is he going
to get you?'

'No!' She was sure of that. 'I'm marrying you.'

Over Alec's dead body, she was. At least, that was the
way he acted. He didn't leave them alone for a minute,
showing up at all hours of the day and night with something he'd 'forgotten to show Michael' or something he'd
'forgotten to say'. He wasn't obnoxious; he didn't have
to be. His persistence was enough.

Libby tried not to let it bother her. Deliberately she
hung on Michael's arm. She kissed his cheek. She
snuggled against him whenever she could. But far from
deterring Alec's onslaught, it seemed only to make it
worse.

'Trying to make me jealous, are you?' he demanded
on the third morning when he had walked in on her
kissing Michael. She had seen him coming up the walk,
had felt that familiar stab of irritation that accompanied
his arrival, and had wrapped her arms around Michael.
Take that, she'd thought, knowing he could see them as
he came up on the porch.

That he had was quite obvious. His glare was intense,
and his usual, 'Hi, how you doin'?' to Michael had a
terse, hard edge to it.

It took him only moments to find an excuse to get her
alone in the kitchen, Michael having gone upstairs to
ask Sam a question that Alec wanted answered.

'I am not trying to make you jealous,' Libby said
tightly, turning away from him, concentrating on pairing
the clean socks in her laundry basket. 'I'm not trying to
do anything to you. You're here. You see what you see.
You take what you get.'

'I think maybe it's about time I did some taking,' Alec
said. 'Is it so wonderful kissing the prof? See if you feel
the same way kissing me.'

And before she could protest he took the socks from her hands and dropped them on the table, then pulled her into his arms, kissing her with a hungry thoroughness with which her kiss with Michael couldn't compare. And her traitorous body loved every minute of it, soaked up every single feeling, while her mind fought for control.

But it was Alec who pulled away, not her. And when he did so, he looked straight at the stairway and gave an apologetic shrug.

'Just making a point,' he said to Michael, his voice almost casual.

Libby hated him more at that moment than she had at any time in the past eight years.

Michael's face was white and expressionless. Only his eyes moved. From Libby to Alec and back again. He looked crushed, betrayed.

She pressed her hand against her lips. 'Damn you,' she said to Alec in a voice as cold as ice. 'Damn you to hell.' And she walked past both of them right out of the door.

She didn't know how far she walked or for how long. Her route was as aimless as her life.

Alec had made his point all right. There would be no marriage with Michael now; she knew that. They all did. She wouldn't even blame Michael if, by the time she got back, he'd already gone.

What, after all, was there to wait for?

Angrily she wiped tears from her eyes and kept walking, wanting to put as much of the island between herself and Alec Blanchard as possible.

When she got back it was almost dusk. Michael was still there, but Libby found him tossing dirty clothes into his suitcase with quick, jerky movements. His face was taut with strain. 'I'm leaving,' Michael said.

'Yes.' She came into the room and sat on the bed, folding her hands in her lap, looking down at them. 'I'm sorry.'

His mouth twisted. 'Me too.'

She raised her eyes and met his. 'I love you,' she said softly, sadly.

He didn't make her feel a fool for saying it. He just smiled, albeit painfully. 'Yeah, I suppose, in a way, you do. But not like you love Blanchard.'

'I don't love Alec!'

'Don't you?' Michael cocked his head, considering this. 'Well, maybe you don't. But you sure as hell feel something for him.'

'I hate him for what he did today.'

Michael sighed. 'Truth hurts.'

Libby shook her head, wanting to cry. 'I wish it could be different.'

He gave a dry half-laugh. 'So do I.' He tossed the last of his clothes into the suitcase and banged it shut. 'I'll be gone in the morning.'

She shut her eyes briefly. 'I—I'll see you in a few weeks.'

He shook his head. 'No.'

'I'll be coming back.'

'Maybe. But don't come and see me. Spare me that.'

Libby looked at him, hurt, but she knew he was right. 'Whatever you want.'

Michael's mouth twisted. 'Whatever I wanted, Libby, it wasn't this.'

They looked at each other, helpless to change anything. The end had come. There was nothing left to say, nowhere else to go.

Sam didn't see why he had to leave. 'You just got here,' he complained when informed the next morning of Michael's imminent departure.

'I have work to do at home,' Michael said.

'Can't 'cha do it here?' Sam asked. 'Mom is.'

'Her work is here. Mine's at home. This was a holiday, Sam, that's all.'

Sam sighed. 'Well, all right.' Then he brightened. 'But we'll see you when we get home.'

Libby said nothing.

Michael said, 'I'll be around.' And if Sam heard the reservation in his voice, he didn't indicate it.

They walked Sam to school together, then continued on towards the dock where one of Maddy's brothers waited to take Michael and a couple of German tourists to north Eleuthera.

Michael tossed his suitcase to Gilbert, then started to climb into the boat. Libby caught his shirt-sleeve. He paused, looking down at her.

Her face felt suddenly hot. 'I just...wanted to say...thank you.'

Michael smiled grimly. 'You're welcome. For what it's worth.'

'It's worth a lot,' Libby said and meant it. 'I'll see you...eventually.'

'I won't wait for you.'

'No. I know that. You know what you need to do.'

'Yes,' Michael said, stepping down into the boat and looking back up at her. His gaze was pitying. 'Do you?'

Libby didn't.

She got nothing done all day, trying to figure it out. Her work lay in a shambles on the table. She couldn't concentrate on it. Her son gave up trying to talk to her. She didn't hear.

'You're missing Michael,' Sam decided.

Libby wished she were. She gave her son a vague, wan smile, and played three games of Chinese checkers with him, proving how very distracted she was by losing all three times.

She was overjoyed when Arthur appeared at the door and wanted to know if Sam could spend the night at his house.

'Can I, Mom?' Sam pleaded.

Libby almost couldn't wait to get him out of the door. She loved him dearly, but she needed some time, some space. She needed a change, to be alone. She smiled, 'Of course you can,' and saw him off with an almost tangible relief.

She came back inside and tried to work. She couldn't concentrate. Not tonight. Wearily she dragged herself upstairs and undressed for bed.

She couldn't sleep, either. She lay there and stared at the ceiling.

The night was hot and sticky, even the fans not cooling the house. Downstairs would be better, she told herself. But even on the sofa, though it was cooler, there was no use trying.

Besides, she thought as she lay there, wide-eyed and weary, for the first time in days she was alone. She had at last the freedom to wallow in the mess her life had become.

She closed her eyes and remembered when it was simple, let her mind rove back to the day when she had first set foot on Harbour Island eight years before.

'It's beautiful,' she'd murmured then. 'Magical.'

And so, for a time, it had seemed.

Well, she thought, she could do with a wave of the wand now. Magic was what it would take to set things right.

What she got was a knock on the door.

# CHAPTER SEVEN

IT WASN'T so much knocking as pounding, loud and erratic.

Libby scrambled to her feet and went to the door, jerking it open before she had time to think.

It was Alec. He loomed over her, very tall, very dishevelled.

'I thought you'd left!'

She gave him an odd, disbelieving look. 'Why would I?'

'Michael left.'

'Thanks to you,' Libby said bitterly.

Alec pushed past her into the room, then turned to face her. 'And a damned good thing, too.'

'I'm sure you think so.' Libby's anger surged in her. Had he come to make sure, then? How could he have thought Michael would take her with him? 'What do you want, Alec?'

'You know what I want.'

'Sam.'

He just looked at her. Then, slowly, he shook his head. 'No, Libby, not Sam. Not just Sam. You.'

She stood with her back to the door, her heart slamming like a jackhammer in her chest as she faced him.

The cool, calm, charming Alec Blanchard who'd harassed her for days was nowhere to be seen. His eyes were bloodshot, his dark hair ruffled. He hadn't shaved. She hadn't seen him since yesterday when she'd walked out of the house. Then he had looked mocking and commanding. Now he looked awful.

'I've always wanted you, Libby. Since the moment we met.'

'Spare me, Alec.'

He shook his head. 'You haven't spared me.' He gave a harsh laugh. 'Especially lately. Lord, how could you throw that bastard in my face day after day?'

'I never—repeat, never—threw anyone in your face! Michael came to see me. He was my fiancé; he had a right to. No one asked you to be here.'

'Was?'

'What?'

'He *was* your fiancé?' Alec's dark eyes were glittering as he repeated her words.

'Was,' Libby said tightly. 'Thanks, again, to you.'

'Was.' Alec tasted the word as if it were ambrosia. He shut his eyes for a long moment, then opened them and looked right at her. 'Thank heaven.'

'Heaven had nothing to do with it. It was entirely your doing. You're a bastard, Alec.'

But Alec didn't seem to hear her. He just muttered, 'Thank heaven,' again and dropped on to the sofa like an anchor settling at the bottom of a fifty-fathom sea.

'Get up,' Libby commanded.

He picked up her pillow and wrapped his arms around it, crossing them over his chest as he glowered up at her. 'No.'

'Go home, Alec.'

He shook his head slowly. 'No.'

'Damn it,' she raged at him. 'Why? Why are you doing this to me? I could understand you being indifferent to me, but to destroy a relationship for me just to get Sam——'

'It has nothing to do with Sam,' Alec said. He gave a savage laugh. 'And to say I'm indifferent—there's a laugh.' He looked up at her. 'I've never, ever been in-different to you, Libby.' The absolute certainty in his tone unsettled her.

Afraid of the look in his eyes, she bit her lip, hesitated. 'Maybe not indifferent, but...' She sighed. 'If it's access to Sam you want, we can... work something out.'

'What do you mean?'

'I... realise that you want to be part of his life. I... I accept that. To a point,' she added hastily, lest he think she was capitulating altogether.

'So you're willing to offer me visitation rights? Is that what you mean?'

'Not... rights exactly. Not in the formal sense. But I—I won't stop you seeing him.'

'Lady, you *couldn't* stop me seeing him!' Alec said harshly.

'I—I——'

'But Sam is only part of it,' he went on. 'Only half. Not even half. What about you?'

'What about me?' Libby said nervously.

'I told you, I want you, too.'

'You don't,' Libby said at once.

Alec scowled. 'Oh, really?' His tone mocked her.

'Really,' Libby insisted.

'How do you figure that?'

'You couldn't. If you did, you could have had me years ago, and you know it. You chose Margo.' She lifted her chin defiantly.

The pain-filled look he gave her only confirmed her suspicions. But he cast the pillow away and lurched to his feet. 'Not now,' he said harshly. 'Now I'm choosing you.'

And what little control he had left completely de-serted him. He reached for Libby, hauling her into his arms.

His kiss was searing, desperate, flaming out of control almost at once. This was not Alec the tender lover of her past, nor was it Alec the lost and lonely soul. This was an Alec pushed beyond endurance, an Alec coming on full force with no holds barred.

At first Libby resisted, fighting him, fighting herself. 'I don't want this!'

'You do. You do,' Alec insisted. 'We both do. It's what we've been dying for since we saw each other again!'

'No, I——'

'Love me, Libby! Damn it, you do! I know you do!'

And Libby knew that, despite her better judgement, despite all her resistance, despite the denial she'd given Michael, it was true.

She loved him helplessly, desperately, foolishly. It didn't matter that he was still in love with his dead wife. It didn't matter that she should have known better. It didn't matter that she'd have been smarter loving any man but Alec. She couldn't stop herself. She didn't know what to do.

Desperately she remembered Michael's words. 'A little hair of the dog that bit you?' he'd asked her that morning after she'd spent the day with Alec at Spanish Wells.

Was loving Alec again the only way she'd get rid of her obsession with him?

Was that what she needed? To share with him the most intimate expression of oneness that two people could share?

Would that quench her thirst for him, satisfy her need?

And what about his need?

Alec's lips were moving on hers hungrily, eagerly. His tongue thrust into her mouth, bringing with it the smoky taste of whisky and something indefinably Alec. His body moulded itself to hers and she felt the hard tension of his arousal. She matched it with her own.

And then she knew there was no other way. Their lives were too entwined to pretend indifference. There could be no indifference where Alec was concerned. To pretend otherwise was to fool herself. If she was going to get over Alec, it was going to be Michael's cure—or nothing.

It only remained to discover which.

Alec was backing her towards the sofa and beginning to fumble with the buttons of her shirt, his mouth still locked on hers.

Libby shook her head. 'No.'

'No?' His voice was raw. 'For pity's sake, Lib——'

'Not here, I mean.' She straightened and pulled away from him, caught hold of his hand, leading him towards the stairs.

He followed her. His eyes never left her, and when they got to the top of the stairs and she led him into her bedroom he pulled her once more into his arms.

His lips brushed against her ear, then traced the line of her jaw and found her mouth once more. She opened it to the thrust of his tongue, wanting it, wanting him. Now, admitting her desire, she felt the restraints fall away.

'Please, Alec!'

'Please?' He smiled. 'Oh, yes. Let me see you, Lib. Let me look at you. It's been so long.'

He lifted her into his arms and carried her to the bed, laying her on it and coming to lie beside her. His fingers shook as they skimmed away her gown and exposed her bare breasts to the moonlight that shone through the open window.

One finger touched her pale skin, making her shiver. He bent his head then, kissing her breasts, laving the nipples, making her bite her lip. She squirmed under his touch.

'Cold?' Alec lifted his head, still smiling.

'Hardly.' Her voice shook. She tangled her fingers in his hair, tugging on it, trying to pull him up so she could kiss him as well. But he wouldn't let her, instead kissing her again, moving from one breast to the other, then going lower until his mouth reached the waistband of her panties.

He rose up then, sitting back on his heels to look down at her. His face was taut, hungry, the skin tight over the bones. His hands came up to touch her shoulders, then skimmed down across her breasts and ribs. His fingers curled around the waistband and tugged.

Libby lifted her hips, letting him remove the panties. But then she was through being acted upon, done receiving.

She caught the hem of his shirt and slid it up, pulling it over his head, then ran her hands down his hair-roughened chest.

His chest was broader than she remembered, the whorls of hair darker, thicker and springier to her touch. She leaned forward and pressed a kiss to the middle of his chest, then touched him with her tongue.

He flinched. 'Libby!'

She smiled, doing to his nipples what he had done to hers. 'Turnabout's fair play.'

'You never used to do things like that!'

'I've grown up.'

He was silent for a moment, rigid under her ministrations, his eyes locked with hers. She knew he was wondering if there had been others. She thought he might ask. But finally he just pressed his lips together and then inhaled long and slow. And when she looked up at him, he just looked at her sadly for a moment, then shook his head.

Libby nearly told him there hadn't been. How could there be, she wanted to ask, when she'd never got over him?

But she didn't, because maybe in the morning she would be over him, maybe in the morning sanity would have returned, and she didn't want to look a fool.

She didn't worry about foolishness now though. She didn't even have time to think.

Alec was kissing her again, at the same time fumbling to undo the button of his shorts. Libby brushed his hands away and did it for him, then eased down the zipper and hooked her fingers over the band of his briefs to pull them off as well.

Alec kicked them away and lay down beside her, his body fitting itself against hers, hard to soft, rough to smooth, and Libby's arms went around him tightly.

For a long moment neither of them moved. It was as though they were readjusting, remembering, reliving. It was, Libby thought, like coming home. As if eight years ago she'd been cast away and since that time had been slowly, desperately, at times without hope, making her way back.

And then she felt Alec's knee nudge hers apart, felt him lift himself so that he was poised over her. His dark face was intent, his jaw rigid as he loomed above her.

He paused then, waiting, tentative almost, and it was Libby who reached up and brought him home. A ragged sigh escaped him. He muttered, swallowed hard, withdrew a bit, then came into her again. And again.

She lifted her hips, meeting him. 'Alec?'

He clenched his teeth, shuddering. 'Oh, lord, Lib! I'm sorry. I can't ... I need ... It's been so long!' He moved more quickly now, desperate for her. And Libby moved with him, never taking her eyes off him, feeling the need building just as he did, feeling the storm peaking inside.

And then it broke, shattering her, shattering him. Shattering most of all every illusion she'd ever had about loving Alec and forgetting him.

She'd never forget this man as long as she lived.

Alec lay trembling on top of her, his back slick with sweat beneath the soothing stroke of her hands.

She shut her eyes then, revelling in the solid weight of his body covering hers, breathing in deeply the tang of salt air, sweat and love, knowing for the first time in eight years a sense of peace. This was what she wanted, what she needed—this hunger, this possession, this man.

She knew that in the morning, whatever else she felt, she would not feel as if she'd got over him.

He slept once briefly, then awoke to love her again. And again. And even when he wasn't making love, he was touching her, as if he couldn't get enough, as if, were he to move so much as an inch away, she might disappear. Did he really care? she wondered. Was there really more to his desire for her than simply sharing sex with her and gaining access to Sam? It seemed like it.

But she was no longer a starry-eyed adolescent. In the clear light of day she knew she was the grown-up she'd hoped—and feared—she would be.

The love was there—probably always would be; she had to admit that now. But her feet were on the ground. If she had no illusions about forgetting Alec, neither did she have illusions about living happily ever after.

He had broken her heart once by leaving her for another woman. Even if she let him into her life, she didn't know when she would ever grow to trust him.

She slept, albeit fitfully, and the moment that she awoke to the sensation of Alec's arm holding her close, his breath tickling her ear, all her worries came back.

'Even better than I remembered,' Alec said, his voice slightly hoarse, but supremely satisfied.

Was it just the sex he wanted, then? Libby turned, meeting his gaze hesitantly.

At her wariness his smile disappeared, his jaw tightened. 'Not for you, huh?'

Libby shook her head, confused.

His mouth twisted with bitterness. 'He's that good, is he, your Michael? Miss him that much?'

Suddenly she knew exactly what he meant and the knowledge made her stiffen. Was that what he thought of her? That she'd spent the last few nights in Michael's arms and, now that he was no longer available, had made a bee-line for Alec?

Abruptly she pulled away and sat up, swinging her feet off the bed.

Alec reached out and grabbed her, pulling her back. 'Oh, no, you don't.'

She struggled. 'Let me go, Alec!'

But he held her fast. 'Not on your life. I can make it good for you, Libby. I know I can.'

She tried to pull away again. 'It's not a contest, damn you!'

'You think I can't measure up? Because I can. I will.'

Libby knew she should fight him. It was sheer folly to give in to his touch. But she was so confused, so lost. Just hours ago she had, for long moments, recaptured the love and the joy of her innocence. She had shared again the purity of that love with Alec. And he had misunderstood.

Now she didn't know what to do, what to think.

But Alec didn't give her a chance to do or think at all. He set about loving her again with an intensity that shattered her. And after a moment's internal struggle, she gave in to it, savouring the sensations that grew inside her as once more she and Alec became one.

Afterwards, spent, Alec lifted his head away from her breasts and looked down at her, his eyes dark and unblinking. And Libby, still trying to gather her soul together from the far corners of the universe, stared back at him.

Neither of them spoke. Then Alec raised himself on his arms and eased away from her, though his eyes did not leave her for a second. He swallowed, then pressed his lips together in a thin line. He didn't say a word.

Libby needed a word—or preferably three. She needed a sign that what they'd shared was really love on both their parts, not love on hers and satisfied lust on his. She tried to read it in his expression, but failed. Silently she begged him for the words to make it all right. But Alec moved off the bed now, silent and unsmiling. He reached for his shorts. Only when he had put them on and was buttoning up his shirt did he finally speak.

'I won't rush you,' he said, his voice even. 'But I will have you.'

And, leaving an open-mouthed Libby behind, he walked out of the room.

So where exactly did they stand? Libby wished she knew.

Admitting that she loved Alec didn't make things any easier. She was more in the dark than ever about the way he felt about her. The 'wanting' of course didn't change. But his behaviour did.

'What's he doing?' she asked Maddy finally after several days had passed. For, though Alec was around every bit as much as he had been when Michael was there—more, probably—he was different.

The aggressive, assertive Alec, who had needled and harassed her since he'd come back into her life, seemed oddly subdued. True, he was with her almost every waking moment, yet he treated her carefully, almost distantly, as if she were a piece of fine china and he was afraid to touch.

Sometimes he ventured close when they were walking. Sometimes he held her hand. And while it was proprietorial, it was still aloof, somewhat hesitant.

It unnerved her. Alec Blanchard was never hesitant. Never unsure. She must be misinterpreting.

But if the Alec of the past few weeks had come into her life like a wrecking bull, determined to destroy her, this Alec was not.

What was going on?

'You don' know, girl? Why he's come a-courtin'!' Maddy laughed.

And, indeed, odd as it seemed at times, Libby could almost believe it was true.

But who was he trying to convince? Libby or himself?

She thought it more likely to be the latter.

He still loved his dead wife. But, because of Sam, he was determined to marry Libby. It wasn't the best foundation for a lifetime's commitment. Yet, wary and hurt though she was, Libby wasn't proof against this new Alec.

She found herself looking forward to the days when he accompanied her on interviews. He usually sat back, listening respectfully, occasionally asking a perceptive question that gave Libby better material than she might have got on her own. Then afterwards he discussed it with her, cracking open the person's story, as it were, making her aware of the nuances and possibilities as she never was on her own.

In the evenings they were usually together, too. He still asked her and Sam to come up to the house for dinner now and then, and as time went on she found herself occasionally inviting him and Juliet to her place as well.

Then he was more the Alec she remembered of eight years ago. But, though he smiled, laughed, and held her hand, there was a distance between them, and he was careful not to so much as kiss her again.

Libby, though she told herself it was just as well, felt perversely bereft.

Don't expect anything, she told herself. He might have asked you to marry him, but it was Margo that he married the first time, Margo whom he loved. Still the courtship—or whatever it was—went on.

One night he got Lois to babysit Juliet and Maddy to take Sam to her house so that they could go to dinner at one of the local restaurants.

There they sat at tables on the lawn, eating spicy conch chowder and the best lobster Libby had ever tasted, while they overlooked the horse cropping the grass at the cricket grounds and listened as, down the hill, the town generator whirred on noisily and just beyond the chain-link fence several motley chickens pecked away.

It wasn't in the least romantic. But tonight Alec was smiling at her as he'd used to, tonight he was holding her hand in his, stroking it gently. And—Libby couldn't help it—it felt romantic to her.

After they'd finished pieces of delicious coconut cake and chatted with Lyman's brother Isaac and his wife, Alec walked her home and there, at last, he kissed her.

It was a gentle kiss. A promise? Libby wondered, and found herself hoping against hope.

'Do you want to come in for a cup of coffee?' she asked hesitantly.

'If I came in it wouldn't be for the coffee,' he said. And, with another quick peck on her lips, he walked away.

Libby stood staring after him, dazed.

The next day he and Juliet accompanied her on an interview, and afterwards, the three of them picked up Sam from school and went for a picnic near the old cannons; and, though their hands brushed and once in passing he nibbled her ear, nothing else occurred.

After they had eaten, Alec flew a kite with Sam. Juliet wanted to help, but the wind off the ocean across the headland blew her long hair into her face, obscuring her vision, making her furious.

'I hate it,' Juliet said irritably, raking her fingers through it. 'Hate it!'

'Get it cut,' Libby suggested, remembering the way it had curtailed her activities at Ben Bay as well.

Juliet looked surprised. 'Cut it?'

'Why not?'

For a moment the little girl looked indecisive. Then she considered Libby's easier to manage shoulder-length hair and the short dark hair of her father and Sam. 'It would be easier, wouldn't it?' she said almost wistfully.

'I think so.'

'Who'd cut it?' Juliet asked.

'I could,' Libby offered before she could stop herself.

'Would you?' The little girl looked at her, eagerness and apprehension on her face.

The apprehension worried Libby. She wondered if she was treading on thin ice. Perhaps Alec preferred Juliet's hair the way it was. The way things were between them, she wasn't sure that she wanted to risk a confrontation. But Juliet's hopefulness prompted her to say finally, 'If your father agrees.'

'Daddy!' Juliet got up and ran to him. 'Daddy! Libby says she'll cut my hair!'

Alec stopped dead. His eyes widened momentarily. He seemed almost shocked at Juliet's words, and Libby felt another stab of worry. His eyes flickered momentarily to meet with hers, his expression unreadable. He seemed about to say something.

Then he smiled at his daughter and reached out to touch her long silky locks. 'Good enough,' Libby heard him say.

Juliet came bouncing back. 'Will you? Will you do it now?'

'I don't have any scissors now,' Libby said. She felt oddly reluctant.

'We can go up to the house.' Juliet tugged at her hand. 'Please.'

Libby glanced at Alec. He didn't look disapproving now, simply curious. Slowly she got to her feet. 'Would you mind?' she asked.

He shook his head. 'Not a bit. Go on.'

The house was quiet, Lois having already done for the day. She'd left a stew simmering on the back of the stove and a note about when Alec should put rolls in the oven. The house seemed lonely and far too large for just the two of them. It made Libby ache to take it over and make it a home.

For the first time she faced the idea squarely and found that it didn't terrify her. In fact she found it oddly tempting. She closed her eyes and imagined what it would be like to cook here, to serve meals to Alec, Sam and Juliet, to sit by the fire in the native stone fireplace on stormy evenings, to climb the narrow spiral staircase and join Alec for a night of love in his bed.

She had never seen his bed, had never been in his bedroom. She shot a fleeting, hungry glimpse towards the stairs now, then dragged her gaze away and made herself focus on the moment at hand.

'Where are the scissors?' she asked Juliet.

'Prob'ly upstairs.'

Libby felt a surge of guilt at the way her unspoken prayer had so neatly been answered. She knew her face was burning. Clearing her throat she said, 'I'll ... look.'

She mounted the stairs quickly, heading straight for the bathroom cabinet, not letting herself look right or left. She opened the drawers one by one, finding the scissors fairly quickly, then turning to go back down.

The bedroom doors stood open. The one closest to the bathroom was obviously Juliet's. Children's toys were visible on the linoleum. The door opposite led into the curtain-darkened master bedroom, a scrupulously neat room with a wide bed.

Unable to help herself, Libby ventured in. Nothing was dusty, but there was an unused feel to the room. There were island-inspired paintings on the walls, bright splashes of colour in an otherwise lifeless room. There were also photographs on the dressing-table. But not recent photographs. She saw Alec's parents on what must have been their wedding anniversary, Alec himself as a little boy with a tooth missing, looking astonishingly like Sam, Alec once more in the cap and gown of high-school graduation.

Libby realised that she had walked into Alec's parents' room, not his. A room which, despite his now being master of the house, he obviously hadn't chosen to move into.

On the far side of the room there was a chest with another photo upon it. Drawn to it, Libby crossed the room and stared at it. It was a wedding photo of Alec and Margo, neither of them looking as radiant as by rights they should have. Alec looked serious, as if the weight of his marital responsibilities was already weighing on him. And Margo—Margo looked scared.

Funny, Libby thought. She wouldn't have guessed.

She picked up the picture and looked at it more closely, remembering the way she'd felt that day, feeling the pain come again almost as strongly as it had hit her then...

She had gone out with him the night after they'd come back from Ben Bay, her hopes high, her expression expectant.

Alec had been remote, his face strained. She had smiled to herself, confident that he was simply working up the courage to tell her he loved her, to ask her to marry him.

They were walking along the beach when he stopped and turned to face her. His jaw was set, hard and tight, and in the moonlight she could see the pulse ticking rapidly at the base of his throat.

He looked down at her, his expression anxious, worried. And Libby looked back at him with the serene confidence of the woman who loved him and knew she could soothe the desperation and worries away.

'I have something to tell you,' he said.

Libby smiled at him. 'Yes?'

'I'm... getting married.'

For a split second she thought he'd meant 'we', thought he'd simply suffered a slip of the tongue. And then, looking at him, she knew he hadn't, knew he'd said exactly what she'd least expected him to say.

She felt as if the words had turned her to stone. She couldn't speak, couldn't even utter a sound.

'Married? To... who?' she managed at last.

He gave an impatient shake of his head. 'To Margo, who else?' His voice was firm, cold.

Margo? Margo Hesse! The name made her blood curdle. It, more than anything, pointed out to her what a fool she'd been.

Margo had been Alec's woman long before Libby had come on to the scene. Libby had thought he was through with her. Obviously she'd been wrong.

She'd been back barely twenty-four hours and he'd asked her to marry him.

The idyll that they had spent together just the day before had meant nothing to him. Margo had his allegiance, his love. He'd been using Libby, that was all. A sop to his loneliness. Lord, what a fool she'd been!

He cleared his throat. 'Better for you, anyway,' he said indifferently. 'You're a kid, Lib. You're going to college, going to meet a lot of new people...'

Libby shook her head slowly, disbelievingly, yet knowing, in spite of her disbelief, that it was true.

You're a kid, Lib. She was also an idiot. A naïve little girl. She wrapped her arms across her breasts, hugging herself as if she was in pain.

In fact the pain was all too real.

'Come on, Lib.' He held out a hand to her. 'I'll walk you back.'

She shook her head fiercely. 'No!'

He made an impatient sound in his throat. 'You can't stay here.'

'What do you care what I do?' She turned away and began walking rapidly down the beach.

Alec came after her, trying to catch her hand. 'Libby! For crying out loud!'

She shook him off. 'Don't touch me! Go away!'

'And leave you here? Not on your life.'

'Why not?

'Because Braden would have my head, damn it.'

She spun and glared at him. 'And that's why? Because you're afraid of Mr Braden?'

'I'm not afraid of Dave Braden. I'm afraid you'll do something stupid.'

'I've already done the stupidest thing I can imagine,' she said bitterly, the tears starting now.

'Libby!'

'Go away!' And she turned and ran from him.

She only saw Alec once more after that, on the day of the reception—the reception she'd deliberately avoided just so such a meeting wouldn't happen.

The Bradens left at the appointed time, taking Tony and Alicia with them, their eyes soft with concern, their minds full of unspoken advice.

'You're sure you'll be all right?' Evelyn Braden asked once more on the way out of the door.

And Libby said again that she would be. 'I'll take it easy,' she promised. 'I'll even nap.'

And she tried. But inactivity got to her after a while. She tossed and turned on the bed, not tired in the least. She couldn't concentrate on the book she tried to read. She was bored by the radio. And while she might have whipped up a batch of cookies at home in Iowa, Maddy didn't like her mucking about in the kitchen here.

At last she sat on the deck twiddling her thumbs, trying to think herself into another world. But over the sound of the waves she could hear a band striking up tune after tune. And now and then laughter and loud voices drifted her way from the reception site at the hotel grounds that sprawled just beyond the trees.

It was going to be the celebration of the century, according to David Braden. 'Surprised he wanted to get married here,' Libby had heard him comment just the day before.

'I think that's what Margo wanted,' his wife had said.

And apparently, Libby thought, whatever Margo wanted, Margo got.

It was increasingly clear to Libby why Alec had dumped her. There was no comparison between Margo and herself. It wasn't only that he'd known Margo longer. Margo was a beautiful talented actress. A striking blonde close to Alec's age. She was sophisticated, worldly, and her father, producer Leopold Hesse, let it be known that he was thrilled with the match.

Libby was young, average-looking, inexperienced. She had neither career nor beauty nor sophistication to recommend her. And Libby's own father, Sam Portman, small-town hardware store owner, wouldn't have cared less.

But Sam Portman would never have to worry, Libby told herself, because the issue of marriage to Alec Blanchard was never going to come up.

The thought of her sturdy, dependable, no-nonsense father brought tears to Libby's eyes. Oh, how she wished he'd been nearby just then. She had always been able to run to him, to find comfort and wisdom in the shelter of his love.

But her father was more than a thousand miles away. And even his love couldn't shelter her from the pain of her own fanciful dreams and subsequent folly.

But that afternoon, when the sounds of the reception became too much to bear, she took a page out of Sam Portman's book of advice.

'Whenever I'm down,' he'd told her more than once, 'I walk it off. I walk and walk and walk. I see the world wide around me. I see the sun, the sky, the trees. And my problems don't seem so overwhelming then. Try it,' he'd counselled. 'You'll see.'

And so Libby left the house, made her way down to the beach and set off determinedly. She walked and she walked. It was nearly dusk by the time she returned, plodding up the beach slowly, wearily, her hair wind-blown, her eyes burning from hours of squinting into the sun. She watched her feet now as she walked, noting the patterns in the sand left by the outgoing waves, forcing herself to recognise the grandeur of the world and the insignificance of Libby Portman's woes. And then she glanced up to see how close she was to the path.

And there he was.

He was perhaps fifty yards from her, down the beach in front of the hotel grounds, and all her concentration, all her resolution fled. He stood in the shallows, his black tuxedo trousers rolled to mid-calf, a pair of black shoes in his hand. He was alone. He was staring out to sea and, just when Libby saw him, he turned his head and looked at her.

Now it will happen, she thought. Now I'll wake up. The nightmare will end. He'll hold me. Kiss me. And the pain will go away.

Alec moved towards her. One step. Another.

Then he stopped. His hands fell to his sides. In the waning light she caught sight of a ring glittering on his finger.

She knew it was no nightmare.

He turned, as Libby did, and walked away.

# CHAPTER EIGHT

'Libby?' Juliet's voice startled her back to the present.

Hastily Libby set the photo back down. 'Coming.' Clutching the scissors, not even glimpsing into the room she knew now must be Alec's, she flew back down the stairs.

Juliet was sitting on a stool in the kitchen patiently waiting. She had a hairbrush in her hand and she presented it to Libby quite solemnly.

Libby took it and began to brush the hair away from Juliet's face. She could see a great deal of Margo in the child now, in her high cheekbones, her delicate jaw. She could see Margo in Juliet's eyes, wide and blue, not a bit like Alec's earthy brown. But most of all she could see Margo in the child's hair. It hung long and straight now, reaching almost to her waist.

'Has anyone ever cut your hair?' Libby asked.

Juliet hesitated, then shook her head. 'No.'

Just as she had feared. Libby's fingers clenched on the scissors. 'Then I really don't think——'

'You've got to,' Juliet said with more determination than Libby had ever heard from her.

'But, Juliet, if no one's ever cut it before——'

'I want it cut. Now.' That was Margo, too. Imperious. Determined.

'Maybe just trimmed?' Libby suggested. 'To even the ends.'

'Short,' Juliet insisted. 'Like yours. Or shorter. So I can play like Daddy and Sam without it always flying in my face.' The imperiousness was gone as quickly as it had come. She turned and looked up at Libby beseechingly.

There was such a need in her. Libby couldn't understand it, just felt it. She didn't know why; she only knew how much it mattered.

She sucked in her breath, took the scissors and began to cut. Long strands of golden hair fell around her feet. And before long the short cap of hair that was left hugged the back of Juliet's neck and brushed against her ears.

It looked nice, and the fact that it did gave Libby more confidence that she was doing the right thing. She had just finished when the phone rang.

She debated for a moment, but when Juliet looked at her expectantly she picked it up. A woman's voice asked for Alec. Her voice was warm and sexy. Exactly the sort of woman she imagined often called Alec. She felt a stirring of jealousy and promptly squelched it.

'He isn't here right now,' she said. 'May I take a message?'

'Tell him Amalia called.' There was urgency in her tone. 'Tell him I need to talk to him right away.'

'Do you know an Amalia?' Libby asked Juliet.

The little girl's eyes brightened. 'Was that Malie?'

Libby nodded.

'She's a friend of my mommy's,' Juliet said, then her expression clouded momentarily. 'She used to come around to see us a lot before Mommy died. She came to see Daddy, too. After. Am I finished now?' Juliet shook her head experimentally.

Libby, dissatisfied with the answers but knowing she'd find out nothing further, nodded.

Juliet bounced off the stool and ran to the bedroom to look in the mirror. Her eyes grew round as dinnerplates as she looked at her new image. She stood absolutely still, as if she couldn't believe the change.

Libby, standing in the doorway, held her breath, letting it out only when Juliet broke into a huge grin.

'Wow! Oh, wow!' Juliet shook her head. The glossy cap of burnished gold swung only slightly. 'I've gotta show Daddy!' And without a backward glance she darted out of the door. Libby could hear her clattering down the steps.

Libby didn't see Alec's first reaction to his daughter's new hairstyle. By the time she got back down to the beach, Juliet was already dancing in and out of the waves, holding the kite-string while Sam offered advice. Alec stood further up the beach, his hands on his hips, watching the two of them.

'What do you think?' she asked hesitantly.

A corner of his mouth lifted. 'It's exactly what she's needed.'

'She said no one had ever cut it before.'

'Margo wouldn't let her.'

Exactly what Libby had been afraid of. 'I didn't mean to—— '

'It's the best thing that could have happened to her. She's letting go, becoming her own person,' Alec said firmly. He reached for her hand and drew her to his side, then bent his head and kissed her. 'Thank you.'

Libby, relieved, revelling in the touch of his lips on hers, smiled back. 'You're welcome.'

But she found herself wondering, is Alec letting go of Margo, too? Would he ever? And if he did, would he ever love her?

He kissed her again, more deeply, and she felt desire begin to stir within her. She knew from the tautening of his muscles and the flush along his cheekbones that Alec was feeling it, too. Hope flared within her.

'Yeah! Awright!'

Libby jerked back at the sound of Sam cheering. Her face flamed as she glanced towards the water and saw

him staring at her, a grin both rapturous and enthusiastic on his face.

Alec laughed and kissed her again. But Libby pulled
away. 'Don't.'

'Why not? He ought to get used to seeing me kiss you.
He doesn't seem to be objecting.'

'Just the same.'

Because she couldn't let Sam hope when she wasn't
sure herself. As much as she knew she loved Alec still,
she didn't know if she could marry him. Not if he only
thought of her as a convenience, a handy woman with
whom to slake his physical desires.

Alec was looking at her, a sad, resigned look on his
face. 'Time,' he muttered to himself.

But Libby wondered if the time would ever come.

'Malie called, Daddy,' Juliet said just then.

Alec frowned and tucked his hands into the pockets
of his shorts. 'What did she want?'

'She said to tell you she called, that she needed to talk
to you,' Libby told him, hoping for an explanation. She
didn't get one.

'Juliet said she was a friend of... of Margo's.'

'Yeah.' Alec didn't answer. His lips pressed together
in a tight line.

Was that all she was? Libby wanted to ask.

But Alec's eyes were on the children. Sam had the kite
now and was running down the beach with Juliet chasing
him, whooping and dashing in and out of the waves.
Alec smiled at the sight of his daughter, so like her
mother even with short hair. 'I do like her haircut,' he
said.

Was it the haircut he liked? Libby wondered. Or the
fact that the pixie-cut made the little girl's cheekbones
and nose all that much more reminiscent of her mother?

That night Alec asked Libby out to dinner.

'To your house, you mean?'

'No. Out. Just the two of us.'

Libby smiled. 'All right.'

Lois watched both children while he and Libby went to Valentine's Yacht Club. They sat at the outdoor bar and watched the sun set over Eleuthera, its last rays painting the line of visiting yachts a vivid blend of orange and pink as they bobbed at their moorings.

He plied her with daiquiris and told her funny stories about the films he'd worked on, exerting himself to be charming. And, though Libby was afraid he was merely doing it because he had to, she couldn't help being charmed.

When it was dark he took her arm and they walked up the hill to a tiny secluded restaurant where the music was soft, the setting tropically elegant, and the food superb. It was the sort of date Libby had once upon a time dreamed about—the man she loved focusing entirely on her.

Afterwards, when she expected him to walk her back home, he led her instead back down towards the yacht club.

'I want to dance with you,' Alec said. 'I've never danced with you.'

As if he had planned it, the moment they walked in, the music shifted from calypso to a softer, more seductive, very danceable bossa nova.

'Perfect,' Alec said and took her into his arms.

No one else was dancing, and for a moment Libby felt foolish. But there was a gentle hunger in Alec's eyes that wouldn't be denied. And Libby dared to hope.

She went willingly into his arms and lifted her own up to hold him close. But not too close. It was very hard.

Still, it was the sort of night she'd dreamed of for years—a night when she and Alec would go out dancing, when he would hold her close and whisper love words in her ear, when he would look as if he couldn't wait to get her alone, and, when at last he did, would love her with all his heart and soul.

'Torture,' Alec murmured against her ear as their bodies touched.

'Yes,' Libby whispered. But the most exquisite torture in the world.

'I want you,' Alec said softly, and she believed, right now, that he really did.

She wanted him, too. But more than simply wanting him, she loved him. She wanted to believe that he loved her. She wanted to trust him, to feel that her own feelings were being returned.

But still, hovering there in the back of her mind, was always the question—would he ever love her for herself? Would he at some future point be able to move beyond Margo? Would he ever come to want Libby for herself and not just because she was Sam's mother?

'I've got to fly to Nassau in the morning,' Alec said suddenly. 'Movie talk. Come with me.'

'I——'

'It'd be perfect.' He paused and looked down into her eyes. 'We could get married.'

The neat way he slipped it in stunned her. Libby swallowed hard. 'I-I don't——'

Alec's smile vanished. 'Still don't want to marry me, huh?' He sounded grim.

That wasn't what she had meant. 'No, I——' How could she explain?

'All right, Libby.' His voice cut through her fumblings like a knife. He rubbed a hand across his face. 'All right, we won't get married. But come with me anyway.'

She looked at him. He looked aloof again, as if a shield had gone down between them. She sighed. 'I suppose Juliet and Sam would like it,' she ventured.

'No kids. Just you and me.' He met her gaze levelly. 'We need to.'

What did he mean? Was this another of his attempts to convince her? Or himself?

Would she ever know if she refused him? Did she really want to refuse him? Well, no. But what if her hopes were raised again, what if she started to believe in him—in them—and it all came to naught as it had before?

'What's life without a risk or two?' Gibb Sawyer had said. He had meant the risks he'd taken on shipboard, but the point was the same. If she didn't go, wouldn't she always wonder if she could have made it work?

'All right,' Libby said. 'Yes.'

Nassau was as fast-paced and frenetic as Harbour Island was laid-back and calm. Libby had never really spent time there before, only passed through it both this summer and the summer she'd come to stay with the Bradens.

To Libby the Bahamas had always seemed sleepy and restful. Nassau was anything but. As they whipped past the posh hotels that lined famous Cable Beach, Libby craned her neck to get a better view. But when the taxi continued, she was glad. Alec himself was glitzy enough. She didn't need a fast-lane hotel as well.

When the taxi finally did come to a stop in front of a two-storey turquoise stucco building with a broad front porch, Libby discovered that they were on a tiny back-street, quieter than most of the clogged thoroughfares, but still close enough to the major downtown attractions for them to walk.

Misgivings assailed her as she stood clutching her bag, waiting for Alec to pay the driver. It seemed like a fairy-tale, and yet she was no longer innocent enough to believe in happy endings. If he'd said he loved her, she would have tried to believe him. But he never had. And even

now, when he'd asked her away for the weekend, he
seemed slightly distant.

Was he wishing it was Margo? she wondered. And
again she wondered if she'd made a huge mistake.

He would expect her to share his bed, she was certain.
After all, she had already done so. But she wanted
more—so much more.

Still, when Alec turned and, smiling, took her arm,
she let herself be led up the steps and into the coolness
of the air-conditioned lobby. It looked more like a living-
room than a reception area. Nevertheless, the woman
there was expecting them.

'Ah, yes, Mr Blanchard. Welcome. Come right this
way. I'll show you to your rooms.'

And, to Libby's amazement, it was *rooms* she meant.
They were next door to each other, granted. But, once
inside, she discovered no connecting door. She had a
room and a key all of her own. Perversely she felt
deflated. So much for hoping that he loved her, that
he'd wanted to bring her so they could iron things out
and make things work.

Dropping her bag and staring around the room,
however, she found it hard to wish she were somewhere
else. It had a moss-green carpet, pale, delicate latticed
wallpaper, and white wicker furniture. Sunlight spilled
through the doors across the wide double bed covered
with a spread in the same pattern as the wallpaper and
banked at the headboard with a row of yellow and moss-
green pillows. Though the room was, thankfully, air-
conditioned, a ceiling fan spun lazily overhead.

Libby walked to the french doors and looked out on
to the balcony, then opened them and went out. Alec
was already there.

'Suit you?'

She gave a hesitant nod, then a more vigorous one.
'It's lovely.'

'I prefer it to the big splashy places.'

'Me, too.'

He gave her an assessing look, then smiled. 'I thought you might. I have a meeting at two with Carras and McKinley at the Sheraton. We can have lunch first if you like.'

He took her to Graycliff, a tasteful, elegant colonial mansion across from the Government House. Libby had heard its reputation as one of the finest restaurants in the entire Caribbean. She'd never expected to try it herself.

'I thought you needed reservations,' she said as they were led into the airy dining-room.

'I got them last week.'

She looked at him curiously. He'd planned this that long ago? 'Before you knew I was coming?'

He smiled crookedly. 'A guy can hope.'

Did he mean it? Libby looked at him closely. For a moment he met her gaze. Then abruptly he turned to the wine list. But Libby smiled, too, finding that a girl could hope as well. And, better judgement aside, she did.

Opening the menu, she focused on it. In the end, though, it didn't matter what she ordered; it was all delicious. But the most delicious part was having Alec all to herself to share it with.

Whatever tension had existed between them since they'd made love and he'd left seemed gradually to dissipate. She didn't know if it was the atmosphere, the food, the wine or the way they smiled at each other. But, for the first time in weeks, Libby started to relax.

Alec seemed to relax, too. The tight lines that had bracketed his mouth ever since he'd made love to her now smoothed slightly. The customary tension in his brow seemed to fade as he smiled at her.

He asked her if she'd ever been to the restaurant before, and when she shook her head he told her about its long colourful history, and its more recent past.

'The Beatles stayed here,' he said. 'And Winston Churchill. Lots of the world's best and brightest.'

Libby was suitably impressed. 'You, for instance?' she teased, for once feeling comfortable enough to do so.

Alec shook his head. 'I've never stayed here. But we used to come here to eat.' He told her he'd come with his parents on his eighteenth birthday, and again on his twenty-first.

'It was a family tradition, coming here for birthdays. My parents even celebrated their wedding anniversaries here,' he grinned. Then the grin faded and suddenly the tension was back. 'They wanted us to. I refused.' His jaw was set, hard and tight.

Libby frowned. Why hadn't he?

But, as always, whenever things had to do with Margo, she sensed a wall there, one which he didn't want her intruding past, one past which she certainly didn't want to intrude.

But, as quickly as it had come, Alec's tension passed. He reached out a hand and touched hers. Libby glanced up, surprised. The look on his face was one of entreaty. She let her fingers curl around his. He smiled.

Around them were the subdued clinks of others' silverware and the muted murmurs of others' conversations. But the world seemed no larger than their table. And, for the first time in years, the harmony between them seemed complete.

It lasted throughout the rest of the meal. It lasted during their walk through the narrow congested streets down to the waterfront where Alec was going to meet Carras and McKinley at their Sheraton Colonial suites and Libby was going to shop along Bay Street. He didn't want to let her go.

'Damn,' he muttered. 'This is the last place I want to go, the last thing I want to do.'

'Don't worry,' Libby said, going up on tiptoe and kissing him. 'We have the rest of the weekend.'

Alec's smile went clear to his eyes. 'We do, don't we?' And though he let go of her hand, he stood in the doorway watching her until she was out of sight.

Libby floated through the straw market, looking a little, daydreaming mostly, finally buying tiny seashell sculptures for Sam and Juliet. She walked as far as the bridge leading to Paradise Island. It was close to four. Alec had said he hoped to be finished by five. She crossed the street and started back.

This side of Bay Street seemed to hold the restaurants, bookshops and bikini shops. Libby nosed through several, picking up a Bahamian history for Professor Dietrich and a rose-coloured two-piece bathing-suit for herself. She hunted everywhere for the perfect thing for Alec, but couldn't find anything suitable. She hovered over a display of men's colognes for the longest time, trying to decide if any of them would suit him. But Alec never wore cologne or aftershave, and she had to admit that she liked him just the way he was.

Shrugging, she hoisted her parcels more securely into her arms and headed out of the shop.

'Libby? Libby Portman?'

Libby looked up, startled. Wayne Maxwell stood beaming at her. 'Fancy meeting you here.' He fell into step beside her. 'Finish your project?'

Libby kept walking. 'Almost.'

'Taking a holiday, are you?'

'Sort of.' She didn't want to mention being here with Alec. It would be just what Wayne was looking for. And she knew too well how Alec felt about reporters. 'Are you?'

He shook his head. 'Of course not. Duty calls.' He grinned. 'But it's always nice when duty calls one to paradise.'

'What duty?' Libby asked him, hoping she might be mistaken.

'Big movie deal going down. Carras and McKinley are here from tinsel town, presumably talking to Blanchard. They're supposed to be having a meeting with the Press, too, afterwards.'

'Today?' Libby asked as they jostled along the pavement.

Wayne shrugged. 'Today, tomorrow...who knows? When the gods get together, the rest of us mortals wait.'

'Interesting.'

'Be a lot more interesting if something juicy would happen. Maybe one of those bimbos who're always hanging around Blanchard will show up. Or, since Carras has split from his wife maybe he'll name her lover. Liven things up.'

'I thought you didn't write gossip,' Libby said, determinedly thrusting away the thought of Alec pursued by bimbos. There hadn't been any on Harbour Island at least.

'Hey,' Wayne shrugged. 'I gotta make a living. Besides, fame makes you fair game.'

Libby shuddered.

Wayne smiled. 'I know. I know. Be glad it's not you.'

One day it could be, though, Libby thought, if she married Alec. Would she be able to handle it? Would Sam and Juliet?

It was something she and Alec needed to talk about.

'Where are you staying?' Wayne was asking her.

'What? Oh, in a little out-of-the-way place. A bed and breakfast, really.'

'All by yourself?'

'Mmm.'

'Good.' Wayne took her murmur for an affirmative. 'How about having dinner with me?'

Libby shook her head. 'I can't.'

'Lunch tomorrow, then?'

'I don't know,' Libby hedged. 'I have a lot to do.'

'I thought you were taking a holiday.'

'Well, I am but...oh, well, why not? Lunch.' She didn't see any way to get out of it short of telling Wayne she'd come with Alec. And after his 'bimbos' comment, she didn't want to do that.

'Great. I'll call for you.'

'I'll meet you. Just name the place.'

Wayne shrugged equably. 'If that's the way you want it. Why don't we eat at the Sheraton? That way I can stay on top of things.'

It wasn't what Libby would have chosen but she didn't see any good reason to give Wayne for objecting. Besides, they were getting close to the Sheraton now, and Libby didn't want to arrive there in Wayne's company. It wasn't just what Wayne would make of her and Alec, but what Alec might think of seeing her again with Wayne.

'Fine,' she said hastily. Then, spying some really outrageous T-shirts in a shop window, she said. 'I really have to stop. I need to get presents for my brothers. I'll see you tomorrow.'

Libby lurked in the T-shirt shop until Wayne had got a block ahead. Then she hurriedly bought two luminous T-shirts with Bahamian slogans for Jeff and Greg and set out for the hotel.

Alec was standing on the steps when she got there. There were no bona fide bimbos in sight, but a group of awestruck teenage girls were hovering about, asking for his autograph, smiling and giggling among themselves. Alec obliged them, but the moment he looked up and spied Libby, he hurried towards her.

'At last.' He caught her arm and tucked her into a taxi in one practiced movement, giving the driver the address of the inn where they were staying. He turned and gave her a long look, a look which made Libby smile.

Alec smiled then, too, and leaned towards her, pulled her into his arms and kissed her hard.

Libby, as hungry for him as he was for her, kissed him back. Her fingers threaded through his thick dark hair, her teeth nibbled provocatively at his lower lip. She felt Alec shudder then pull back, grinning wryly.

'Are you going to still feel this way when we get to the inn?' he asked her, his voice hoarse.

Libby gave him a demure smile. 'I think I might.'

And when Alec walked her to the door of her room, deliberately she drew him in.

They loved that night with the joy they'd loved with eight years before. And when they awoke and loved again, though Libby waited for him to pull away as he had the last time, he stayed with her, held her in his arms and slept. Smiling, happy for the first time in so long that she couldn't remember, Libby slept, too.

It felt as if the barriers had finally crumbled, as if fears had finally died.

And the next morning, when Alec was supposed to get up for more meetings with Carras, he didn't get out of bed. He wrapped her in his arms, hugging her close.

'Damn Carras,' he muttered, kissing her lips, her nose, her cheeks. 'Damn McKinley. I'd far rather stay right here.'

Libby smiled, sleepy and sated. 'Me, too.' She pulled away slightly and looked up at him. 'But duty calls.'

'Damn duty, too,' Alec said, burying his face in her hair.

By the time they finally got out of bed, showered and dressed, pausing as they did to touch, to stroke, to linger, Alec was late.

'I hate this. I feel like a heel running out on you,' he groused.

Libby shook her head. 'Nonsense. You knew you had to do this when you invited me along.'

'But I didn't know we'd be doing *this* as well.' His gaze went speakingly to the rumpled bed.

Libby just smiled. 'I'll come along,' she said. 'I can do some more shopping. I don't have anything for my mother yet.'

Alec held out a hand to her. 'Come along, then.'

This time he insisted on taking her up to the suite to introduce her to Carras and McKinley. Libby looked around nervously, expecting to see Wayne, worried about what he'd think if he saw her with Alec, worried about what Alec would think if he thought she was talking to Wayne. Happily Wayne was nowhere to be found.

Carras and McKinley both fitted her stereotypes of studio executives, a Tweedledum-Tweedledee duo who puffed cigars and wore expensive silk suits. But if they thought Alec had dredged up a hick-from-nowhere as his latest girlfriend, they were too polite to say so.

'So you're why Alec's been champing at the bit,' Ross McKinley said and winked at her. But there was nothing lewd in the wink, and Libby smiled at him gratefully. 'Can't say I blame him,' he went on.

Alec hugged Libby hard against him. 'And she's why I'm splitting today,' he told both men. 'So if you want this flick to fly, let's get going.'

Libby left them to it and went back down to the lobby and outside. The day was hotter and more humid than the one before, but she scarcely noticed. Her head and her heart were both filled with memories of the night before, of this wonderful feeling of harmony, of rightness between herself and Alec.

She almost felt like telling Wayne. But she wouldn't. It was too new, too precious, too perfect. She wanted to hug it to herself for just a while longer. And before she ever said anything to the Press, she and Alec would have to talk to Sam and Juliet. There were things that had to be explained to them.

But even those explanations didn't daunt Libby now. Together, she thought, smiling, she and Alec could manage. He might not have said yet that he loved her, but she was beginning to trust at last that he did.

She was still smiling, still glowing, when she met Wayne for lunch an hour later.

'You look marvellous.' The frank admiration on his face told her he meant what he said.

'The climate agrees with me.' She took her seat in the restaurant he steered her into and smiled across the table at him.

Wayne mopped his brow. 'I'll say. Or,' he added hopefully, 'maybe it's the company. Listen. I've got an exclusive interview with Carras this afternoon, but how about going out with me tonight?'

Libby shook her head. 'I have to go back to Harbour Island. This was just a getaway.'

'Sure you wouldn't like to take a longer one? I could hang on a bit longer. Maybe Blanchard will do something outrageous, elope with an actress or some damned thing.'

Wouldn't he be amazed if he knew? Libby thought, smiling to herself. She shook her head. 'I can't.'

Wayne didn't give up as easily as she might have hoped. After he'd badgered her a bit more during lunch, and when she hoped to escape him after, she found he had the afternoon free and was quite willing to tag along after her. When the time came for her to meet Alec, she still hadn't got away from him.

'I don't want to keep you from your work,' she said somewhat desperately.

'No problem. Where are you going now?'

'I——' she cast about for a destination that was close enough to the Sheraton that Alec wouldn't think she'd left but that would perhaps bore Wayne into declining to accompany her '—I need to buy some postcards and...and stamps.'

Wayne took her arm. 'I know just the place.'

He manoeuvred her across the street, dodging cars and taxis and led her straight towards the Sheraton itself. 'Gift shop right through here,' he said. 'Bought stamps there yesterday.'

There was nothing Libby could do but follow. She chose cards at random. Wayne hovered at her elbow, offering suggestions, waiting while she paid for them, reminding her when she forgot the stamps. They were heading out of the door and she was beginning to despair of ever shedding herself of him when suddenly he looked up.

'Carras!' he exclaimed. 'And McKinley. And Blanchard.' He turned and gave Libby a smacking kiss. 'Gotta run, sweetheart. Duty calls.' And he was gone.

Libby, praying that Alec hadn't seen them, hovered back inside the gift shop until she saw Carras, beaming, bear Wayne away with him for the 'exclusive' he'd been promised. Alec stared after them. McKinley was still talking to him, but Alec didn't seem to be attending. Then Libby saw McKinley clap Alec on the back and grin. Alec just nodded.

Libby wondered if he'd been that distracted throughout their entire meeting. She smiled. She didn't know whether she hoped so or not. Slipping the stamps and cards she'd purchased into her bag, she headed out through the door to meet him.

'Hi. I'm not late, am I?'

Alec shook his head. 'No.' He didn't smile at once. He looked worried.

'Hey,' Libby took his arm. 'It's not as bad as all that.'

Alec scowled. 'What's not?'

'Whatever happened in your meeting,' she said, smiling. Then, when he still didn't smile, she grew concerned. 'Is something wrong? Didn't it go well?'

'What? Oh, the meetings? Yeah, they were all right.'

'You finished, then?'

'Yeah.' He looked down at her, his eyes searching.

And Libby, knowing what he was looking for, reached up and put her arms around him, kissing him soundly.

For a moment it seemed as if Alec was going to resist. Then, at last, he returned her kiss. He even took her back to her room to make love to her one more time before they left.

This loving was more intense than that they had already shared. Alec seemed almost desperate in his need for her. And Libby shared that desperation. And afterwards she felt she was the happiest woman alive.

Even marriage, she was certain, couldn't bring them closer than they were now.

And when they got back to Dunmore Town and Alec walked her from the dock up the narrow streets to her house, she didn't want to let him go.

'I wish you could stay,' she whispered as they stood on the porch, arms around each other, foreheads touching.

Alec kissed her longingly, then pulled away, though his lips lingered a fraction of an inch from hers. A corner of his mouth lifted ruefully. 'And you think I don't?'

'You will soon,' Libby said. It was a commitment. A promise.

'Mmm.' He kissed her again with everything that was in him.

'I'll see you in the morning,' Libby said.

He never came.

# CHAPTER NINE

NOT ever.

Libby waited. And waited.

She got up the next morning, humming to herself in anticipation, hardly able not to sing out the news to Sam. She made his breakfast, still humming snatches of songs. She walked up to school with him, less for the walk than in the hope that she would catch her first glimpse of Alec coming up the street. When she didn't see him, she went home, philosophical, still thrilled.

She made the beds and transcribed the tape of the interview with Gibb Sawyer. She made coconut bread from the recipe Maddy had given her. The whole time she did so her hearing was attuned to the lightest footstep on the porch, the slightest knock on the door.

By noon she'd stopped humming. She even found that she was scowling as she folded the laundry and mended a tear in Sam's shorts.

Don't, she warned herself. There would no doubt be plenty of times when Alec would be late, when something would come up to delay his return. Being a film director was not a nine-to-five job. She would have to get used to it.

She tried.

But by three that afternoon her imagination had run away with her. She wondered if he'd fallen ill, if something had happened to Juliet while they'd been gone. She conjured up disasters, fires, muggings.

When Sam came in from school she pounced. 'Did you see Juliet yesterday?'

He shook his head. 'Nope.' He dropped his books on the couch and settled down at the table with a glass of milk and a slice of coconut bread.

'Not at all?' Libby pressed.

'Huh-uh.' Sam took a huge bite of the bread.

Maybe she *was* sick, Libby thought desperately. Or hurt. Maybe when Alec had got home last night, something had happened to her. That had to be it. Otherwise he would have come. Libby wished for the thousandth time that day that she had a phone.

'Did you see her at all over the weekend?'

Sam chewed his bread. 'Saturday. She an' some lady were walking towards Hill Top when Arthur an' me were comin' up from the dock.'

Libby frowned. 'What lady?'

Sam shook his head. 'Dunno. Can I have another piece of bread?'

Absently Libby cut him one, her mind flipping over possibilities with the speed of a humming-bird's wings. 'Come on,' she said. 'Let's go for a walk.'

He shrugged, then stuffed the last of the bread into his mouth, drained his glass of milk and got to his feet. He didn't ask where they were going; he seemed to know.

'Are you worried?' he asked her.

'A little,' Libby admitted. 'Alec was supposed to come by this morning, and he didn't. So I thought something might've happened to Juliet.'

'You like Alec a lot, don'cha?' Sam asked, running to keep up with Libby's hurried strides.

'I'm very...fond of him.'

She loved him. She was willing to admit it now. To Alec. To Sam. To everyone.

But last night on the flight home she'd promised Alec that when they told Sam who his father was they'd be together. And they'd tell Juliet together, too. That was the way it would be from now on. So she just gave Sam a reassuring smile and hurried on.

As soon as they came around the bend in the road she began to look for Juliet, to listen for her shrill voice, to catch a glimpse of her golden hair.

She saw no one, heard nothing save the ocean's muted surge against the sand. She let herself in at the gate, leaving Sam to latch it while she went directly to the door and knocked loudly.

It seemed to take an age for the sound of footsteps to be heard. And when the door opened, Libby began, 'Oh, Alec——' But it was Lois standing there.

Lois smiled broadly. 'Come in. Come in.'

Libby hesitated, then did so, glancing around for signs of disaster. There were none. 'I—er—is—I mean, I was expecting Alec. Looking for him, that is.'

Lois frowned. 'Mr Alec, he's not here.'

Libby felt relief flicker through her. 'Oh, well, I must have missed him. Maybe he was going to our house the beach way while we were coming up the road.'

Lois shook her head. 'Not on the island, I mean. He's gone.'

'Gone?' The relief died, a quick swell of panic drowning it. 'Where? Why?'

Another shake of Lois's dark head. 'Don't know, really. Didn't say.'

'He just *left*? What about Juliet?'

'She, too. She an' Miz Webster. They all go.'

'Miss Webster?' Libby's fingers gripped the doorjamb.

'You know, Miz Webster. Miz 'Malia Webster. The actress.'

'I don't want to talk about it.' Deliberately Libby bent her head over the cake-mix she was stirring, wishing herself oblivious to her mother's concern.

'I think you ought to,' Christine Portman said, her eyes expressing a blend of love and worry as she stood in the kitchen of Libby's home and watched her only daughter try to ignore her the way she'd tried to ignore everyone for the past week. 'I think you *need* to.'

'There's nothing to say.' Libby went on stirring. Nothing she *wanted* to say, at any rate. And she could hardly expect her parents to nurse her through yet another folly with the same man.

That was, perhaps, the hardest part—being made a fool of twice. Falling in love with a rogue at the age of eighteen might be excusable on grounds of naïveté. Falling in love with a rogue at the age of twenty-six was foolishness. And there were no words left to describe the idiocy of a woman who fell in love with the same rogue twice!

'It was Alec Blanchard again, wasn't it?'

Libby sighed, knowing that the time had come, that her parents' patience had worn through. They had been tolerant as could be when she'd returned two weeks ago, looking like the ghost of Christmas past. They, better than anyone, knew how distraught she'd been when she'd come home eight years ago.

But they'd been tolerant for two weeks now, hovering, concerned, but silent. Now, Christine seemed to be saying, enough was enough.

Libby knew her mother was right. She just wished the truth didn't make her sound like such an idiot. If only there was some way she could have disguised the source of her distress.

They hadn't connected the first time with the second until Sam had started talking about his friend Alec.

Then both Libby's parents' eyes had widened, their jaws had dropped, and they'd looked to her for confirmation. She hadn't said a word.

She couldn't stop Sam talking, of course. No one could ever stop Sam talking. The most she could do was hope that eventually he would find something else to say.

Eventually he did. The longer they were home and the more time he spent with his friends, the less every sentence began with 'Alec said...' or 'My friend Juliet...'

Still, hearing less about Alec didn't give Libby the reprieve she'd prayed for. On the contrary, she thought about him all the time. She might have left Harbour Island, but she hadn't left Alec behind.

She had tried to behave in a mature, rational manner when she'd first heard Lois's words. So she hadn't fled Harbour Island at the first inkling that once more Alec had gone off with another stunning actress, though with every fibre of her being she wanted to.

Instead she'd thanked Lois politely and walked slowly and sedately back across the island to her home, Sam firing off volleys of questions as he dogged her heels.

Libby hadn't answered any of them. She had had too many of her own.

Why? she'd asked herself over and over. Why had he done it? What did it mean? Was it all some perverse game he was playing? Did he care at all? How did Alec really feel about her? About Sam?

And to every question she had only one answer: she didn't know.

She had hoped it might be a mistake, that Lois had somehow got things wrong. But a day had passed with no word, and then another.

Sam's questions hadn't abated, but Libby's patience had. It was no mistake. And she'd be a fool to sit and wait forever. She'd be a fool if she even waited another day.

She had her work more or less finished. And what she hadn't got by now, she'd do without.

Alec knew where she lived. If he wanted her, he could find her. Not that she wanted him. Not after the way he'd behaved.

'What we going to tell Mr Alec?' Maddy grumbled when Libby bade her goodbye.

Tell him to go to hell, Libby thought, but she only shook her head. She had nothing left to say.

She still didn't. For if she'd thought she was leaving precipitately, if she'd thought there was the slightest chance that she had made a mistake, the magazines she'd seen in the supermarket just yesterday had proven her right.

There on the front page of two of the more sensational journals were pictures of Alec and Amalia Webster disembarking from an aeroplane in Los Angeles, a pinch-faced Juliet in the background. One had the headline 'ALEC AND MALIE RETURN FROM BAHAMIAN LOVE NEST.' The other asked more bluntly, 'IS THIS THE WOMAN WHO WILL TAKE MARGO'S PLACE?'

Stricken, Libby just stared at them. She felt a hand come down on her shoulder and, starting, turned to look straight into Michael's concerned eyes. It was the first time she'd seen him since she'd come back.

He looked briefly at the headlines, grimaced, then looked back at her. 'I'm sorry, Lib,' he said.

Libby closed her eyes. 'Thanks.' What else, after all, could she say?

Michael, bless him, didn't ask a thing. He offered to buy her a cup of coffee, she declined, and he nodded understandingly. 'I'll see you home.'

She didn't object. She didn't have the strength.

Michael was quiet the whole way, and when he let her out at her front gate he looked at her, concerned. 'You'll be OK?'

'Of course.'

'I'll see you around, then. We'll have supper.'

Libby nodded yes. But they wouldn't. She could never go back to Michael now, and both of them knew it.

'It was Alec, wasn't it?' her mother asked gently now. 'Your Alec.'

'He's not *my* Alec,' Libby said fiercely. She swiped at her eyes as tears threatened. 'And there are a million other Alecs in the world besides him.'

'Yes,' Christine said reasonably, 'but not another one who could do this to you.'

And that, Libby had to admit, was true.

'I'm fine,' she said stubbornly. 'Yes, I ran into Alec there. But that's irrelevant. I finished my project right on schedule. Early in fact. So I came home. What's the big deal? What's everyone worried about?'

Christine touched her arm, turning her so that Libby had to look into her mother's eyes. 'You, Libby,' Christine said softly. 'We're worried about you.'

How could you fight a mother's concern, a mother's love? How could you deny it when you needed it so much? Libby couldn't. She shook her head helplessly, the pain of the past week overwhelming her. The tears she'd held at bay brimmed over at last.

'I feel such a fool. I fell in love with him,' she whispered, agonised. 'I fell in love with him all over again.'

Christine put her arms around her daughter. 'Oh, my dear.'

Libby shuddered and sucked in a deep breath, getting a grip on herself. 'I should have known better. I shouldn't have trusted him. He said he loved me. He said he wanted to marry me. He said...'

But there was no point in repeating what Alec had said. His actions, once again, she told her mother, had spoken louder than his words.

'It will take time, that's all,' Libby assured her.

She had got over Alec before. She had gone on to have a happy, productive life. She still had her home, her family, her son—everything she'd had before she'd gone to Harbour Island in June. If she had done it once, she could do it again.

'Sam's coming,' Libby's mother said. 'He and Pop must have finished the tree-house.'

Sam's raving about Juliet's tree-house had convinced his grandfather and uncles that a similar one in the oak tree in their back yard would be worth the effort. Ever since they'd come back, the building had gone on. Libby suspected that part of her father's willingness stemmed from his perception that keeping Sam busy and distracted would give Libby some space and time to come to terms with what had happened. She was grateful.

She made a point of spending time each day doing something special with Sam, too.

She had done that from the day they'd returned. She knew Sam would miss his afternoons with Arthur, going fishing with Lyman, playing with Juliet. So she made up her mind to provide him with some new memories to replace the old ones.

One day they'd baked a cake from scratch. Another they had gone for a hike and explored the caves in one of the county parks. Yesterday, after she'd come back from the supermarket, the stories about Alec still spinning in her head, she had shoved them aside, smiled at her son and asked him if he wanted to go swimming.

Today, as Sam came puffing up to regale them with the latest tree-house stories, Libby asked if he wanted to go for a bike ride.

'Sure. But you gotta see the tree-house first.'

Libby and Christine followed him back up the lane and along Elm Street to inspect the tree-house. It was every bit as nice as the one Alec had built.

But after Libby and Sam had started out on the bikes, Sam confided, 'I like it a lot. But I liked Alec's better.'

Libby didn't answer. She just said, 'Race you to the fence-post.' And Sam, no proof against a challenge, took off pedalling.

They met Michael coming out of the library. 'Going somewhere?' he asked.

'We're riding out to Ericson's,' Sam told him, mentioning the farm just outside town which they often used as a turnaround point.

'Warm day for a ride,' Michael said.

Libby nodded.

'Mind if I ride along?'

Libby opened her mouth.

'Just for company. No strings,' Michael said quickly. 'You look as if you could use a friend.'

'I don't want to presume,' Libby said. 'I can't——'

'I know that, damn it,' Michael said. 'Just friends, all right?'

Libby nodded. He unlocked his own bike and, with Sam in the lead, they pedalled down the road.

It was a hot day, beastly and humid—the sort Iowa was famous for. The sort that made Libby long for an ocean breeze like the ones she'd left behind. Bike-riding was not one of her better ideas, and going right out to Ericson's place had been a mistake. She was vastly relieved to turn around.

Sam's stamina had increased over the summer. He no longer lagged behind when they rode. In fact, now, as they pedalled homeward, the humidity was affecting her more than it was her son.

'C'mon, Mom!' Sam yelled, half a block ahead of her.

Libby waved at him, marvelling at his unflagging eagerness. She wanted to drop.

'Go on ahead,' she called to him as they approached their lane. 'You can get the iced water ready. I'm ready for it,' she said to Michael. 'How about you?'

He shook his head. 'Committee meeting at three. I gotta go home and grab a shower first.' He rode with her to the gate, then paused.

'There,' he said. 'See? That wasn't so bad, was it?'

Libby shook her head. 'I just don't want you to get hurt again.'

'I won't,' Michael promised. He winked at her, shoved away from the curb and vanished up the lane.

Libby got off her bike and pulled it up on the curb, then reached to unlatch the gate.

'Allow me.' The voice was gruff. Hoarse. Alec's.

Libby ran over her foot as she stared.

'Mom! Look, Mom! Look who's here!' Sam appeared right behind him, grinning for all he was worth.

She supposed she should have expected it. He had, after all, come to explain his defection the first time. Why should this one be different? She gritted her teeth.

Alec didn't say a word. He looked none too happy either, though what he should have to be unhappy about she didn't know. Steeling her emotions, she gave him a brusque nod and got off her bike. He opened the gate and stood back while she wheeled the bike past him into the yard.

'He was standin' on the porch when I got here,' Sam told her, bouncing alongside. 'How come you left? Where'd you go? Where's Juliet? Did you bring Juliet?' he asked Alec.

'Not this time,' Alec said, answering only the last. 'I came alone.'

'How come?' Sam looked up quizzically.

'I needed to talk to your mother.'

''Bout what?'

'That's between your mother and me.' Alec looked searchingly at Libby. She wondered if he expected her to agree. Fat chance, she thought. This was his idea; let him fob Sam off.

She pushed her hair back off her sweaty forehead. She needed to be cool and calm to deal with Alec. Trust him to show up now when she was a wreck!

'Are you stayin' for supper?' Sam asked. 'We're having spaghetti.'

A corner of Alec's mouth lifted. 'Sounds good.'

Sam cocked his head. 'So you are stayin'!'

'We'll see,' Alec said.

'Why don't you run over to Grandpa and Grandma's for a bit?' Libby suggested to her son.

Sam gave both of them a long assessing look, as if he wondered whether he dared leave them alone. Then, apparently deciding that his presence wasn't going to settle things, he shrugged and started for the gate, then turned back. 'Where is Juliet?'

'I left her with a friend. Amalia Webster.'

Who else? thought Libby. Any hopes that Alec might have come to sweep her into his arms died right there.

It was to be just another explanation, like last time. Or—and here a shaft of pure terror shot through her— had he come to try to get her to agree to let him take Sam with him as well?

The thought rooted her right where she stood. She felt by turns cold and hot; her mind focused with blinding clarity on the horror of the notion one second and spun out of control the next.

She watched Sam go, a small reluctant figure who kept glancing back as if one or the other of them might disappear. She made herself smile and shoo him on, all the while promising him silently that she'd never let him go with Alec, not over her dead body.

Libby turned and walked straight past Alec up the steps and into the house. 'You needn't have bothered,' she said.

He strode after her, letting the screen door bang behind him. 'That's it, huh? Just wait until my back is turned and run off?'

Libby whirled, aghast, anger flaring. 'What the hell do you mean by that?'

'Just what I said. I'm gone three days and you vanish. Not a word. Not a message. "She just left, Mr Alec. I don' know why."' He mimicked Maddy's soft Bahamian accents. 'Well, damn it, I want to know why!'

Over her shoulder Libby shot him a disbelieving stare. 'You're the one who left, Alec,' she said finally, her mouth twisting. 'Not me. Think about it.'

'I can explain.'

'As you "explained" last time?' Libby couldn't mask her bitterness.

Alec raked his fingers through his hair. 'This time is not last time. Damn it, Libby! Listen to me. You have to listen to me!'

Libby spun around and glared up at him. 'I do? Why? Eight years ago you didn't listen to me!'

A spasm of pain flickered across Alec's face. He swallowed. 'I know that,' he said quietly. He bowed his head for a moment, then raised it and looked right at her. 'I'll regret that every day of my life.'

And Libby knew that, no matter what he told her now, about that at least he was telling her the truth.

For all the good it did, she reminded herself, steeling herself against him.

Alec rubbed a hand down his face, rocked back on his heels, then tucked both hands in his pockets. 'Lord, what a mess,' he said under his breath.

'Yes,' Libby agreed tightly.

He sighed, shaking his head. 'Even now I don't know what I could have done differently. With regard to us, I mean.' The look he gave her was sad now, rather than angry. 'Obviously I should never have married Margo.'

'You loved Margo,' Libby reminded him.

'The hell I did!'

Libby goggled at him, shocked to the core. 'What?'

'I did not love Margo.' He bit the words out.

'But...but you must have! You...you married her...' Her voice faded.

'You don't only marry for love,' Alec said grimly.

It had just been a fling, then? Libby didn't know how she felt about that. Did it make things better or worse? 'You married her because she was pregnant?'

'Yes.'

'I don't see the difference, then,' Libby said frankly. 'Marrying her or marrying me. We were both pregnant. She just got there first.'

'I loved you,' Alec said quietly. 'And...' he paused, his gaze flickering around the room for a moment as he ran his tongue over his lips and drew in a long breath '...I did not get Margo pregnant.'

Libby's eyes met his slowly, doubtfully. 'What are you saying?'

'Exactly what you imagine I'm saying. Juliet is not my child.'

Libby just looked at him.

Alec repeated it. He looked at her steadily, his eyes dark and unreadable.

'But you said that's why you married Margo!'

'It is.' Alec began prowling the kitchen again. 'But I never had an affair with her. I wasn't ever interested in her in that way.'

'All those magazine stories——'

'Hype,' Alec said succinctly. 'And red herrings. Margo didn't want anyone to know who she was really involved with. Daddy didn't approve.'

At sea, Libby didn't know what to say. 'Who...?' she began finally, then stopped. It was none of her business.

'Clive Gilbert.'

It took a moment for the name to register. 'Clive— the stuntman? The one who...?'

'Who was killed,' Alec finished for her. 'Doing my work,' he added. 'I told you it was a mess. That day when we came back from Ben Bay and Margo showed up—that's when I found out she was pregnant. She was distraught. Frantic. She'd never been particularly stable, and Clive's death had devastated her. Then she found out she was pregnant.'

Alec's fingers clenched on the counter-top. He stared, unseeing, out of the window. 'She knew her father would flip,' he went on. 'He didn't think Clive was good enough for her. He'd forbidden Margo to have anything to do with him. That was why she was planting stories about being seen with me. Then, when Clive died and she found out she was expecting his child, she was desperate. She came to me.'

Libby stared straight ahead, trying to make sense of it all. Outside in the treetops cicadas hummed. The paper-boy whacked the newspaper against the door.

He hadn't loved Margo? He'd married her out of kindness? Did that mean——?

'I did what I thought I had to do,' Alec said heavily. 'I told her I'd marry her. She said OK.' He gave a wry grimace. 'It wasn't OK, right from the very start. She didn't love me; she loved Clive. I didn't love her; I loved you.'

'You...' Libby began, but she couldn't repeat the words he'd just uttered.

'I loved you,' Alec said forcefully. Then he shrugged. 'But I didn't think you loved me. Not really. I mean, you were a child, and I'd seduced you. You had your whole life ahead of you. You had plans—to go to college, to get your degree, to become someone your family could be proud of. You had it all worked out. I thought it was the best thing to do—marry Margo and let you go.'

*Dear Lord,* Libby thought. 'But that note you wrote. It was so—so hard. "Forget me. You can be sure I'll forget you."' Even now quoting it was painful.

Alec winced. 'I didn't know!' he said, anguished. 'I couldn't string you along, damn it. It wasn't true. I didn't forget you, but I wanted you to forget me. I was married, for better or worse. And believe me, it was "worse" right from the start.

'The whole time she was pregnant, Margo was in mourning for Clive, but she kept herself under control. Before Juliet was a week old, she was getting drunk. I think reality finally hit her. She'd hoped for a miniature Clive—a baby who looked just like him, who could replace him. And instead she got Juliet—a girl, and one who looked very much like her.

'Plus, Juliet wasn't an easy baby. She was colicky, fussy. She cried a lot. So did Margo. It was not a happy time.'

Alec flexed his shoulders and shook his head. 'It went downhill from there. She didn't even want to see Juliet about half the time. And the other half, she fawned all over her, got obsessed by her. The hair, for example. She'd never let her cut it. There were other things, too. Malie kept an eye on her, which was a good thing because I had damned little time to.'

Malie. He said her name so casually. But it made Libby realise that all she was getting was an explanation, not a declaration of undying love. She bit down on her lip and waited. It made sense, all of it. But it didn't mean things were going to work out.

'I was busy, running all over the damned globe shooting movies,' Alec went on, 'and at the same time trying to keep things together at home, trying to make things at least look as if they were working.'

He sighed. 'A losing proposition, as it turned out. Stupidest thing I ever did. Margo didn't want me, and I didn't want her. It didn't take long before she began to look for replacements for Clive.'

'You mean...?' But Libby couldn't make herself voice the question.

'I mean she started taking lovers,' Alec said flatly. 'Most of them were one-night stands. But the last one was a bit more. He was a reporter.'

Libby blanched.

Alec smiled bitterly. 'You begin to understand. His name was Jerry Corson——'

'The man who died in the crash with her?'

'The man Margo wanted a divorce to marry. He could be Juliet's father, she told me. I said no.' He sighed. 'I don't know. Maybe it was pure selfishness on my part. I hope not. I told myself I wasn't doing that to Juliet. I might not have been there always, but I was reliable at least. And I loved her.' He swallowed hard and shook his head. 'Margo ran off with him anyway. That's what they were doing when they were killed.'

'But I heard she and a reporter were coming to meet you!'

'No use raking up more muck when they were both dead. But it wasn't true,' Alec said heavily. 'I had been in Mexico, filming. I was coming home to Santa Barbara through LA. Margo and Jerry just happened to be heading toward LA when Jerry lost control of the car.' He shut his eyes, his face bleak. 'I can only thank heaven that Margo decided I was right about Juliet and left her at home for me. Otherwise she'd have died, too.'

'Dear lord,' Libby whispered, sickened at the thought.

'Exactly,' Alec said. 'So there you have it, the whole sordid mess. The only good thing to come out of it was Juliet.'

'You don't regret Juliet, surely?' Libby couldn't help saying.

'No. I love her. And for her sake I can't regret marrying Margo. But I will always regret that it took me away from you,' he went on. 'I used to console myself by thinking that at least I'd protected you, that even if my life was a mess, yours had been what you'd planned. What a noble bastard I was!'

'Margo probably needed you more than I did,' Libby allowed, and knew that, for all her regrets, it was true.

'I don't know,' Alec said, his voice toneless. He didn't look at her.

'And...and Juliet probably needs you more than Sam. She's a wonderful little girl,' Libby said earnestly.

Alec nodded. 'I used to think she was more a part of me than I could imagine any child of my own flesh and blood could be. But that was before I met Sam,' he said, his mouth quirking with a sort of wry bitterness, 'and now I don't know.'

'Y-you can see Sam,' Libby offered in a low voice after a long moment, 'when you want to.' She gazed out of the window, refusing to meet his eyes.

He didn't speak, but she heard him swallow, heard the floor creak under the shift of his weight. 'See Sam?'

'You have the right,' Libby admitted, slanting him a glance.

He had sagged against the counter, his expression bleak. 'So, that's it, then?' His voice sounded hollow, lifeless.

'It?'

Alec rubbed a hand down his face. 'I knew, of course. I just . . . hoped. Hell!' He turned and stared unseeingly out of the window. 'Is it Michael? Or Maxwell?'

Libby stared at him. 'Is what Michael or Maxwell? Maxwell who?'

'Wayne Maxwell. *Your* reporter.' Alec's bitterness was apparent. 'Which one is it? Which one are you going to marry?'

Libby stared at him, stunned. 'I don't know what you're talking about.'

'Oh, don't give me that,' Alec snapped. 'I've heard it all before from Margo. She denied Corson, too. But I saw her with him, the same way I saw you with Maxwell. And Michael just left here!'

'You saw Maxwell? When?'

'In Nassau,' Alec said. 'At that gift shop. I came out of the hotel with Carras and McKinley and I saw you through the window with him. He kissed you.'

Libby didn't even remember the kiss. 'I had lunch with him.'

'You didn't say!'

'I knew how you felt about reporters.'

Alec's jaw clenched. He shook his head stubbornly. 'Maybe not Maxwell, then. But Michael. You were engaged to him.'

'Yes, I was,' Libby said tightly. 'And we all know how you took care of that.'

'For all the good it did me.' He sighed. 'Serves me right, I guess. Fool that I am, I thought I could get you back.'

He wanted her back? What about Amalia?

'So he wins out in the end, does he?' Alec asked.

For an instant Libby was tempted to take refuge in the lie. It would be so much easier on her pride to let him think that, to let him walk away feeling rejected for once.

But she couldn't. She'd never been anything but honest with Alec no matter how much pain it had caused her. She would have to be honest one last time.

'I'm not marrying Michael. I'm not marrying anyone.'

'Why not?' Alec demanded.

What did he care? 'Because I don't love him,' Libby flared at him, goaded at the inquisition. 'I won't marry a man I don't love!'

'Would you have married me?'

Libby turned away from him, looking down into the sink. The question reverberated in the room.

She heard Alec move, felt the heat of his body close behind hers, then felt his fingers lightly touch her shoulder. Libby flinched.

'Never mind, Lib. You've made yourself clear. You don't have to spell it out for me.' He bent his head then and touched his lips to the nape of her neck. Libby held herself rigid, tortured at his touch.

At last Alec drew back, and Libby felt moisture there, trickling down the back of her neck.

She turned her head and stared.

He stepped back. 'A just revenge, Lib. I walked away from you. Now you can walk away from me. But at least know this. I love you, Lib. I always will. But I understand. I really do.' He faltered. His voice cracked. 'I—I would like to see Sam sometimes...if...if you can bear it. I...oh, hell, Lib.' He turned and walked quickly towards the door.

Libby saw the tears, heard the words, and couldn't understand either, could scarcely believe either.

He loved her? What about Amalia Webster? What about him leaving with her? What was he saying? She couldn't let him go—not without trying to understand, not without admitting her own love for him.

'Alec!'

His hand paused on the doorknob, but he didn't turn around.

Slowly Libby walked across the room. She halted only inches from his back, noting its rigidity, the tension almost vibrating through him. The ridge of his spine stood in stark outline against his shirt. Lightly Libby touched it, trailing her finger down its length.

Alec winced.

'I love you, too, Alec,' she whispered.

For a long moment he didn't move, didn't breathe, didn't say a word. Then he turned around slowly, the look on his face incredulous, desperate. 'Lib?'

She nodded jerkily.

'Then——' his voice was anguished '—then why did you leave? I came back and you were gone. No word. No nothing.'

'Amalia Webster,' Libby said simply. 'It was just like before. The actress from afar, swooping down, changing everything.'

Alec groaned. 'No.'

Libby pressed on. 'Yes. It was in the magazines I saw just the other day. You and Malie...'

He said a rude word. 'No. Lord, no. First of all, the magazines are nothing but hot air. It isn't true, any of it. Please, listen to me. Malie is Clive Gilbert's sister!'

Libby blinked. 'Clive's sister?'

Alec nodded. 'Yes. She's the only one besides me who ever knew about Margo and Clive. She's also the only one who knew that Juliet wasn't my child. She always told both Margo and me that we should tell Juliet the truth, that we shouldn't lie to her. She said Juliet had a right to know who her real father was. She said her family had a right to know about Juliet. Sound familiar?'

Libby sighed. 'Like Sam.'

Alec nodded grimly. 'Exactly. And we didn't want to listen either. Margo was too unstable, and I—I thought it would crush Juliet. She had enough to contend with.' He sighed. 'I never thought about Clive's family. Until this summer.'

He paused, drumming his fingers on the counter-top. 'Then I realised how much I would have missed if I'd never found out about Sam. I hated that, but it made me think. I wanted you to tell him who I was, and when you wouldn't what could I say? It was precisely what I'd been saying to Malie for years.'

'She called you,' Libby remembered.

'Yeah. Her mother was going in for heart surgery. Malie wanted to tell her about Juliet, give her someone to live for. I still hesitated. It still seemed like opening a huge can of worms. I pointed out the problems, the pitfalls, told her that her mother would have other grandchildren. And she said, "Does one child ever replace another?"' His eyes met Libby's, his expression wry. 'You know the answer to that.'

Indeed Libby did. She reached out and took hold of Alec's hand.

His thumb rubbed along her wrist. 'I told her I'd talk to Juliet, tell her the truth. I was going to talk to you about it when we were in Nassau, but at first I was too busy loving you, and then——' his jaw tightened '—there was Maxwell.'

Libby groaned.

'I didn't know what to think. I didn't know if you were interested in him, if you might tell him...'

'I wouldn't have——'

'But I didn't know! I thought I was making progress with you, getting you to love me again. But I didn't know. You were so cool, sometimes——'

'I was afraid.'

'I was, too.'

Alec, afraid? It hardly seemed credible. But a look at his face told her the truth of what he was saying. Libby squeezed his hand and his fingers tightened around hers.

'Malie was waiting when we got back to Harbour Island. Her mother was desperate to see Juliet before she went into surgery. It would take two days. Three at most. What could I do?'

He had done, Libby realised, the only thing he could.

'I could hardly send her to California with just Malie. It was a shock. She was confused. I couldn't say go without me or she'd have thought I wasn't only telling her she had another father, but that I was abandoning her. I wanted to tell you. I got up at dawn to come down and talk to you. And then I thought, no, I couldn't burden you with it. It was my problem. I'd started it by marrying Margo. If I was going to come to you and try to make you love me again, I had to do it with everything settled. I got back three days later and you were gone.'

'Oh, Alec.' Libby's eyes burned, her throat felt tight.

'So I figured I was right all along, that you hadn't ever got over Michael, that I'd got rid of him, but not your love for him.'

'Whatever made you think it?' Libby asked him.

For a moment he didn't answer. Then, colour running high along his cheekbones, he muttered, 'When we made love.'

'What are you talking about?'

'Afterwards. You weren't exactly thrilled.'

She hadn't been. She'd been worried because her love had been as strong as ever and she had no idea what it was that Alec felt. 'I didn't know why you'd done it,' she said simply.

Alec stared. 'Because I loved you! Why else?'

'Because you wanted Sam and thought that a bit of sex might be nice, too.'

Alec said a rude word and kissed her fiercely. 'I love you,' he said firmly. 'Then. Now. Always.'

'And I love you.'

'Thank heaven.' Alec's kiss was long and hard, possessive, hungry. He clung to her like a man lost, now found, once adrift, now saved.

'I thought you hated me,' he whispered against her hair. 'When I opened the gate for you today I thought I was a fool to have come. You looked at me as if you wished I were dead.'

'I thought you'd come for Sam. To take him from me.'

'Never. I love Sam, but I came for you.' Alec stroked her hair away from her face. 'I don't want to be away from you ever again.'

'Nor I you.' And Libby lifted her face to his, kissing him again, revelling in the feel of the hard warm length of him against her. 'You are the other half of my soul.'

Neither of them spoke then, just held each other, savouring the moment, the peace, the possibilities. The past, painful as it had been, no longer mattered.

'You know,' Libby said finally, tipping her head up to look into his eyes which were still unusually bright, 'I want to regret it all. I want to have those eight years back, to have spent them with you. But I love Juliet, and I can't. I just can't be sorry.'

Alec nodded. 'I know. I feel the same.' He touched his lips to hers, gently, longingly. It was a kiss full of love and infinite promise, and Libby met it with one of her own.

There was a slight noise just beyond the screen door. Alec and Libby pulled apart and looked around.

Sam stood there, a grin as wide as the Mississippi on his face. 'Does this,' he asked happily, 'mean we're marrying Alec after all?'

OVER THE YEARS, TELEVISION HAS BROUGHT
THE LIVES AND LOVES OF MANY CHARACTERS INTO
YOUR HOMES. NOW HARLEQUIN INTRODUCES YOU
TO THE TOWN AND PEOPLE OF

One small town—twelve terrific love stories.

GREAT READING...GREAT SAVINGS...AND A FABULOUS
FREE GIFT!

Each book set in Tyler is a self-contained love story; together, the
twelve novels stitch the fabric of the community.

By collecting proofs-of-purchase found in each Tyler book, you can
receive a fabulous gift, ABSOLUTELY FREE! And use our special
Tyler coupons to save on your next TYLER book purchase.

Join us for the fourth TYLER book,
MONKEY WRENCH by Nancy Martin.

*Can elderly Rose Atkins successfully bring a new love into
granddaughter Susannah's life?*

---

# FREE GIFT OFFER

To receive your free gift, send us the specified number of proofs-of-purchase from any specially marked Free Gift Offer Harlequin or Silhouette book with the Free Gift Certificate properly completed, plus a check or money order (do not send cash) to cover postage and handling payable to Harlequin/Silhouette Free Gift Promotion Offer. We will send you the specified gift.

## FREE GIFT CERTIFICATE

| ITEM | A. GOLD TONE EARRINGS | B. GOLD TONE BRACELET | C. GOLD TONE NECKLACE |
|------|------------------------|------------------------|------------------------|
| # of proofs-of-purchase required | 3 | 6 | 9 |
| Postage and Handling | $1.75 | $2.25 | $2.75 |
| Check one | ☐ | ☐ | ☐ |

Name: _____

Address: _____

City: _____ State: _____ Zip Code: _____

Mail this certificate, specified number of proofs-of-purchase and a check or money order for postage and handling to: HARLEQUIN/SILHOUETTE FREE GIFT OFFER 1992, P.O. Box 9057, Buffalo, NY 14269-9057. Requests must be received by July 31, 1992.

PLUS—Every time you submit a completed certificate with the correct number of proofs-of-purchase, you are automatically entered in our MILLION DOLLAR SWEEPSTAKES! No purchase or obligation necessary to enter. See below for alternate means of entry and how to obtain complete sweepstakes rules.

### MILLION DOLLAR SWEEPSTAKES
#### NO PURCHASE OR OBLIGATION NECESSARY TO ENTER

To enter, hand-print (mechanical reproductions are not acceptable) your name and address on a 3"×5" card and mail to Million Dollar Sweepstakes 6097, c/o either P.O. Box 9056, Buffalo, NY 14269-9056 or P.O. Box 621, Fort Erie, Ontario L2A 5X3. Limit: one entry per envelope. Entries must be sent via 1st-class mail. For eligibility, entries must be received no later than March 31, 1994. No liability is assumed for printing errors, lost, late or misdirected entries.

Sweepstakes is open to persons 18 years of age or older. All applicable laws and regulations apply. Sweepstakes offer void wherever prohibited by law. Prizewinners will be determined no later than May 1994. Chances of winning are determined by the number of entries distributed and received. For a copy of the Official Rules governing this sweepstakes offer, send a self-addressed, stamped envelope (WA residents need not affix return postage) to: Million Dollar Sweepstakes Rules, P.O. Box 4733, Blair, NE 68009.

✂ HP2U

## ONE PROOF-OF-PURCHASE

To collect your fabulous FREE GIFT you must include the necessary FREE GIFT proofs-of-purchase with a properly completed offer certificate.

(See inside back cover for offer details)

# Harlequin Presents®

## Coming Next Month

Available in June wherever paperback books are sold, or through Harlequin Reader Service:

In the U.S.
P.O. Box 1397
Buffalo, NY
14240-1397

In Canada
P.O. Box 603
Fort Erie, Ontario
L2A 5X3

## *GREAT TEMPTRESSES* WORD SEARCH CONTEST

Harlequin wants to give romance readers the chance to receive a fabulous GE SPACEMAKER TV, ABSOLUTELY FREE, just for entering our *Great Temptresses* Word Search Contest. To qualify, complete the word search puzzle below and send it to us so that we receive it by June 26, 1992. Ten entries chosen by random draw will receive a GE SPACE-MAKER TV, complete with 6.5″ B & W screen, a swivel bracket for easy hanging and built-in AM/FM radio!!!

```
B  E  T  T  Y  G  R  A  B  L  E  L  R  S  D
T  K  E  I  R  A  H  A  T  A  M  N  C  N  E
L  Y  M  E  L  L  E  S  S  M  E  H  L  R  E
L  E  A  S  A  L  O  M  E  B  E  E  E  C  O
A  C  D  O  O  W  A  N  W  H  Q  L  O  U  R
C  E  O  E  B  N  Z  L  E  A  R  E  P  J  N
A  F  N  G  R  H  I  R  A  L  O  N  A  B  O
B  X  N  Z  A  X  A  P  M  I  N  O  T  T  M
N  Y  A  C  G  Z  D  O  R  L  J  F  R  B  N
E  S  I  V  A  D  E  T  T  E  B  T  A  I  Y
R  M  O  D  T  S  U  V  C  D  J  R  V  O  L
U  R  E  A  E  P  Q  W  H  H  L  O  Q  Y  I
A  M  J  C  R  W  A  O  T  S  E  Y  H  I  R
L  A  D  Y  G  O  D  I  V  A  B  R  X  C  A
S  S  C  A  R  L  E  T  T  O  H  A  R  A  M
```

| | | |
|---|---|---|
| MARILYN MONROE | HELEN OF TROY | LAUREN BACALL |
| DELILAH | LADY GODIVA | BETTY GRABLE |
| GRETA GARBO | SALOME | SCHEHERAZADE |
| MADONNA | BETTE DAVIS | MAE WEST |
| MATA HARI | CLEOPATRA | SCARLETT O'HARA |
| CHER | | |

*Please turn over for entry details*

# HOW TO ENTER

All the names listed below the word puzzle are hidden in the grid. You can find them by reading the letters forward, backward, up and down, or diagonally. When you find a word, circle it or put a line through it. Then fill in your name and address in the space provided, put this page in an envelope and mail it today to:

Harlequin *Great Temptresses* Word Search Contest
Harlequin Reader Service®
P.O. Box 9671
Buffalo, NY 14269-9671

YOU COULD GET A FREE GE SPACEMAKER TV, JUST FOR PLAYING!

NAME _____

ADDRESS _____

_____

CITY _____ STATE _____ ZIP CODE _____

H2MAY2

Rules
1. All eligible contest entries must be received by June 26, 1992.
2. Ten (10) winners will be selected from properly completed entries in a random drawing from all entries on or about July 1, 1992. Odds of winning are dependent upon the number of entries received. Winners will be notified by mail. Decisions of the judges are final. Winners consent to the use of their name, photograph or likeness for advertising and publicity in conjunction with this and similar promotions without additional compensation.
3. Winners will receive a GE Spacemaker TV, with a total retail value over $100.00.
4. Open to all residents of the U.S., 18 years or older, except employees and families of Torstar Corporation, its affiliates and subsidiaries.